PUFFIN

SURVIVE!

SNOW
TRAP

It was getting dark, the snowstorm was rapidly becoming a blizzard . . .

Suddenly Lee stopped. The ground ahead ended abruptly.

'What's up?' Tom had to shout to make his voice heard above the howling wind.

'We're on the edge of a cliff, I think.' Lee crouched down and squinted. The ground fell away steeply. He shivered. If he hadn't noticed it, they'd have plunged over.

'What are we going to do?' Tom asked despairingly.

'We'll have to go back.' Lee's heart sank at the thought. Despite their weariness, they'd have to climb back up this steep slope and find another way down. 'We'll have to be careful, too,' he added. If they slipped while they were above this precipice, they'd slide straight over the edge.

'We're lost, aren't we?' Tom said, his voice sharp with fear.

SURVIVE!

SNOW TRAP

Jack Dillon

PUFFIN BOOKS

For everyone at Oakfield Middle School

Special thanks to Liss Norton and Ian Locke

PUFFIN BOOKS

Published by the Penguin Group
Penguin Books Ltd, 27 Wrights Lane, London W8 5TZ, England
Penguin Putnam Inc., 375 Hudson Street, New York, New York 10014, USA
Penguin Books Australia Ltd, Ringwood, Victoria, Australia
Penguin Books Canada Ltd, 10 Alcorn Avenue, Toronto, Ontario, Canada M4V 3B2
Penguin Books (NZ) Ltd, Private Bag 102902, NSMC, Auckland, New Zealand

On the World Wide Web at: www.penguin.com

Penguin Books Ltd, Registered Offices: Harmondsworth, Middlesex, England

First published 2000
1 3 5 7 9 10 8 6 4 2

Created by Working Partners Ltd, London, W6 0QT

The moral right of the author has been asserted

Set in Bembo

Made and printed in England by Clays Ltd, St Ives plc

British Library Cataloguing in Publication Data
A CIP catalogue record for this book is available from the British Library

ISBN 0–141–30445–6

CHAPTER ONE

'I wish our bags would hurry up,' Lee Saunders said impatiently, running a hand through his blond hair. He and Tom Cavendish, his best mate, had been standing by the luggage carousel at Lyons airport for nearly thirty minutes. Their snowboards were already on their trolley but their holdalls were nowhere to be seen.

Apart from them, only two families with young children and a middle-aged couple were still waiting. Tom, a lanky, sandy-haired fourteen-year-old, sighed. 'Just about everyone else has got their stuff and gone.'

Lee nodded. 'At this rate, we're going to

1

spend the whole week in the airport,' he said, smiling wryly. He was half a head shorter than Tom and was dressed in baggy combats and a loose-fitting black jumper. 'Jeff'll be miffed if our bags have got lost,' he added. 'I think he'd prefer us to lose our snowboards.'

'Would he?'

'Oh, yeah. My brother *hates* snowboarders.'

Tom frowned. 'Why?'

A pair of smart, grey suitcases appeared on the carousel. The boys watched them go past. The middle-aged man lifted them off.

'Jeff reckons snowboarders are irresponsible and selfish.' Lee laughed. 'If he had his way, the sport would be banned.'

'He does know we snowboard, doesn't he?'

'Not yet. But he's about to find out.'

Tom groaned. 'That means you two will spend the whole week arguing.'

'No we won't.' Lee sat down on the edge of the trolley. 'The last time she phoned him, my mum gave him a lecture on brotherly love – so he'll *have* to be nice to me.'

Tom pulled a face. 'I can't see that making any difference. I know what you two are like when you get together. And if he hates snowboarding he'll have plenty to go on about.' He buried his face in his hands in mock dismay. 'Why did I ever agree to come?'

'We're not *that* bad.'

Tom hooted with derision. 'I've never known anyone argue as much as you two do. Your mum and dad must have been over the moon when Jeff got this instructor's job in a ski school. I bet your house is really peaceful since he's been in France.'

Lee stood up. 'I'll be on my best behaviour. I won't do or say anything to wind him up.' He grinned. 'Except snowboard, of course.'

Their bags appeared at last. They dragged them off the carousel and made room for them on their trolley.

'Come on, let's go and find Jeff,' Lee said.

Jeff was waiting in the arrivals lounge. He looked like a bigger and older version of Lee, though his hair was slightly blonder from being out in the Alpine sun for weeks on end. He smiled and waved as Lee and Tom came towards him. 'I was beginning to think you'd missed your flight.' Jeff shook Tom's hand and gave his brother a hug. 'Everyone else came through but …' He broke off and his smile faded as his gaze fell on the blue, padded

3

snowboard cases. 'That's not *your* luggage, is it?'

'Yep.' Lee winked at Tom. 'Here we go,' he said under his breath.

'Mum didn't tell me you were bringing snowboards.'

'Didn't she?'

'No.' Jeff glared at Lee. 'I suppose you asked her to keep quiet about it.'

Lee shook his head. 'Not me.' He struggled to keep a straight face.

'I can't believe it,' Jeff said. 'My own brother. Snowboarding! What's wrong with skiing, for heaven's sake?'

'Nothing. I love skiing. I just happen to like snowboarding even more.'

'But you're a brilliant skier,' Jeff cried. 'And you're good, as well, Tom, aren't you?'

'We're not too bad at snowboarding either,' Tom said. 'We've had a few lessons on a dry ski-slope. We can do all the basic stuff – so we won't be a nuisance to anyone.'

Jeff snorted. 'Snowboarders are always a nuisance. They go too fast. They ...'

'Shouldn't we get going?' Lee said. 'It'd be nice to get on the slopes today, if we can.'

'So you can get in everyone's way?'

Jeff stalked off. Lee and Tom followed.

'Why did I come on this holiday?' Tom wailed, steering the trolley round a group of noisy French children and their harassed-looking leaders. 'It's going to be a nightmare.'

Lee shrugged. 'Hopefully he'll be teaching most of the time, so we won't see too much of him.'

Jeff stopped and waited for them to catch up with him. 'I thought you were in a hurry to get to Chambeau,' he said irritably.

'Coming, brother dear,' Lee replied.

'Those stupid jumps are the worst,' Jeff complained, crashing his car down into second gear as the traffic slowed. 'Snowboarders try jumping over things, make a mess of it, fall over – and the next thing you know, they're zooming down the mountain, out of control.'

Lee looked at the line of cars ahead, wishing the hold-up would clear. Jeff had been going on about snowboarders ever since they'd left the airport, three-quarters of an hour ago, and Lee didn't think he could bear being stuck in the car with him much longer.

He turned his head and surveyed the snowy

mountains speckled with clusters of dark pine trees. The sight cheered him. In another hour or so they'd be on the slopes, trying out their snowboards on real snow for the first time.

'And what about snowboarders' hats?' Jeff went on. 'They're so brightly coloured they hurt your eyes.'

Lee swivelled round in his seat and grinned at Tom, sitting behind him. He'd bought a new hat himself. A lime-green-and-orange jester's hat. 'Don't tell him about my hat,' he mouthed.

Tom nodded.

'What are you two whispering about?' Jeff demanded.

'Nothing.' Lee turned back and looked out at the sky. It was a dull, leaden grey. 'Do you reckon it's going to snow?' he asked, trying to get Jeff on to a safer subject.

'Could be. We've had a lot of snow lately. Much more than usual. Let's hope it doesn't interfere with the skiing.'

'How can snow interfere with skiing?' Tom asked. 'Skiers need snow.'

'The authorities close the slopes if too much snow falls in too short a time. It creates an avalanche risk.'

Lee didn't say anything, but secretly he hoped it would snow a bit more. Snowboarding was best on fresh, powdery snow. He looked at the sky again. It was satisfyingly dark, as though there was plenty of snow up there just waiting to fall.

They reached Chambeau at last. It was a new resort, not far from Val Thorens, and was perched high on a mountainside. Wooden chalets, their roofs and balcony rails covered thickly with snow, lined the road. As they passed through the centre of the village, Lee saw bars, restaurants and souvenir shops. A narrow area of pavement had been cleared in front of them and the snow was piled up in massive heaps beside the road. Lee was astonished by the sight. 'There's an incredible amount of snow,' he said. He'd been skiing every year since he was seven but he'd never seen snow as deep as this.

'I told you,' Jeff said. 'It's been a bad year. We've had the heaviest snowfalls in twenty years. The slopes at some of the other resorts were closed all weekend.'

'Were they all right here?' Lee asked anxiously. He hated the thought of coming all this way and not being able to snowboard.

'Yes. Our slopes aren't particularly steep, so the problem wasn't so great.'

They turned a corner and came upon a group of children throwing snowballs. Jeff sounded his horn and they skipped out of the way, waving. Jeff waved back.

'Are they pupils of yours?' Tom asked.

'Two of them are. The other three are in the beginners' class. Dominique teaches that.'

Dominique was Jeff's girlfriend. Lee was looking forward to meeting her. He couldn't imagine anybody voluntarily spending time with his brother, so he was keen to see what kind of person she was. She'd have to be a saint to put up with Jeff.

They drove up a gentle hill, then Jeff steered into a car park in front of a bar. Groups of people, well wrapped up against the cold, were sitting at tables outside, drinking from steaming mugs.

'That's our chalet.' Jeff pointed to a small wooden chalet further up the hill. Lee looked it over eagerly, glad to have arrived at last. The chalet had a sloping roof, green shutters and a first-floor balcony that appeared to run right round the building.

They climbed out of the car and stood for a moment, breathing in the cold mountain air. Above them the ski slopes stretched up and up, a broad expanse of brilliant white dotted here and there with dark conifers, rocky outcrops and descending skiers. Higher still, the grey sky, weighed down by snow, seemed to be resting on the mountain peaks.

'I don't like the look of that sky,' Jeff said. 'I'm not sure you'll get out on the slopes today, after all.'

Lee flung open the car boot. 'Let's get our stuff inside quick, then,' he said. 'You never know, it might only snow lightly for an hour or two.' He pulled out the snowboards. 'Give me a hand, Tom.'

They carried the luggage towards the house, crunching over the well trodden snow that covered the pavement. An area of path by the front door had been cleared and they stepped down on to it. Jeff unlocked the front door and they went inside.

'Your friend really owns this chalet?' Lee asked, looking round the cosy living-room. A fire burnt behind a fireguard at one side of the room and a burgundy settee and two matching armchairs were arranged around it.

At the far end of the room stood a dark wood table and four chairs. There was a staircase against the back wall.

'That's right.' Jeff moved the fireguard, took a poker from the hearth and stirred the fire, making it flare up brightly. 'He lives in England, but he comes over here to ski. Luckily for you, he couldn't make it this week. You wouldn't have been able to stay otherwise, because the ski-lodge I live in is usually full of instructors and tour reps.'

Lee took off his boots so that he wouldn't tread snow into the thick carpet. 'We'll get a few things out of our bags and then go straight out on to the slopes, shall we, Tom?'

'Yeah, brilliant,' Tom replied enthusiastically.

'That's right, you go and terrorize everyone on the slopes,' Jeff said sarcastically. 'Your room's the first door on the left at the top of the stairs.'

The bedroom the boys were sharing was painted pale pink. 'Yuk!' Lee dumped his bag on the bed nearest the window. 'This is disgusting!'

'We won't be in here much,' Tom said, 'except at night – and we'll be asleep then.' He frowned. 'Unless you and Jeff keep rowing all week. If you do that, *I'll* be up here most of the time.'

Lee opened his bag and pulled out his jester's hat. He put it on and admired his reflection in the mirror.

'Don't let Jeff see you in that,' Tom groaned, delving into his bag. 'You'll only start him off again.'

Lee pulled the hat off and flung it on the bed. He changed into the loose, brown, waterproof trousers and soft, black-and-white snowboard boots that he'd bought especially for this holiday. He smeared sunscreen over his face, put his goggles on the top of his head and tossed a few essentials into his backpack.

Finally he rubbed some wax on to the bottom of his board so it would run smoothly. 'Are you ready?' he asked. He could hardly wait to snowboard on real snow.

'Almost.' Tom pulled his padded gloves out of his bag. 'Don't forget your hat.'

Lee picked it up and stuffed it inside his coat where Jeff wouldn't see it. They went downstairs.

A pretty, dark-haired girl, aged about nineteen, was standing by the fire, warming her hands. She turned and smiled at them, her brown eyes twinkling.

'Hello. Jeff's in the kitchen making coffee.' She spoke with a French accent. 'You must be Lee and Tom.'

Lee returned her smile. 'Yep. I'm –'

The girl held up a hand to silence him. 'I can guess. You're Lee. You look just like your brother.'

Lee flashed her an indignant look. 'I'm nothing like Jeff.'

Tom laughed. 'Yes you are! You're *exactly* like him. Same blond hair, same blue eyes, same broad shoulders, same bad temper –'

'All right, all right. You don't have to remind me.'

The girl laughed too. 'So this must be Tom.'

'That's right.'

'Are you Dominique?' Lee asked incredulously. He thought she seemed much too nice to be Jeff's girlfriend.

'Yes. Jeff's told me lots of things about you.' She lowered her voice and pointed to the snowboards, 'I see you're snowboarders.'

'I'm surprised Jeff didn't mention it,' Lee said.

'He did, actually. He said quite a lot about it while you were upstairs unpacking. That's why I told him I'd like a coffee. It was the only way to get some peace,' Dominique said, grinning. She glanced at the door that led to the kitchen, then she beckoned to the boys. They drew nearer to her. 'I'll give you some lessons, if you like,' she whispered.

'You're a snowboarder?' Tom asked in astonishment. 'Does Jeff know?'

'Of course. I run classes for holidaymakers.'

'Doesn't he go on at you the whole time?'

She smiled ruefully. 'Now and then.'

'Coffee's nearly ready,' Jeff called from the kitchen.

'We won't stop for coffee, thanks, Jeff,' Lee said. 'Do you want to come out with us now, Dominique?' he wondered hopefully.

She nodded. 'I'll go back to the ski-lodge and fetch my board. It's not far. Wait for me by the drag lift at the top of this road.'

Jeff came out of the kitchen carrying two steaming mugs of coffee.

'Oh, Jeff, sorry. I'm going out snow-boarding with Lee and Tom,' Dominique said apologetically. 'I won't have time for a drink after all.'

Jeff set the mugs down on a low table and pulled a face.

Dominique laughed and caught his hand. 'Come with us. I'm sure you'd enjoy it.'

Lee gawped at her. If Jeff came with them he'd spoil the whole afternoon.

Jeff sank into an armchair close to the fire. 'No way,' he said firmly.

Lee breathed a sigh of relief.

'Anyway,' Jeff went on. 'I've got to cook dinner.'

'Cook dinner?' Lee echoed, his heart sinking. Jeff was a terrible cook.

'What's wrong with me cooking dinner?'

'Nothing,' Lee said hurriedly. 'I'm sure it'll be delicious.'

'Quite right. Be back by six,' Jeff said. He took a couple of lift-passes out of his pocket and handed them to Lee. 'You'll need these.'

'Thanks, Jeff,' Lee said. He felt a momentary pang of guilt. Jeff had really put himself out for them. He'd borrowed this chalet and had moved out of his room in the ski-lodge for the week. He'd even got them to send him photos so that he could organize their lift-passes in advance. But, so far, they'd barely said a civil word to each other.

'And mind you don't get in the way of the skiers,' Jeff said sharply.

Lee's guilt evaporated. Why did Jeff always have to be so unreasonable? There was nothing wrong with snowboarding.

They went out.

'I'll get my board. See you by the lift, then,' Dominique called as she headed down the hill.

'Yeah.' Lee put on his jester's hat, then he and Tom set off along the snowy road, heading uphill. The sky looked darker than ever. Putting all thoughts of Jeff out of his mind, Lee looked up at the mountainside, already imagining himself skimming over the snow. 'This is going to be a great holiday,' he said.

CHAPTER TWO

Lee stood at the top of the nursery slope. Below him, novice skiers were moving cautiously downhill. To either side of them were dozens of snowboarders. Most of them were sideslipping or traversing in a gingerly fashion down the mountain. A few were moving more quickly, gliding backwards and forwards through a series of accomplished turns.

'I'm going to start by traversing,' Lee said, glancing round at Tom and Dominique. 'Just to get the feel of boarding on snow.'

Dominique nodded approvingly. 'Good idea. What else can you do?'

'Sideslipping,' Tom said. 'And heelside and toeside turns.'

'We haven't done any jumps yet,' Lee said. 'But I want to get the hang of ollies while we're here.'

Dominique smiled. 'It sounds as though you're doing well. I should think you'll be jumping in a couple of days. For now, though, you could concentrate on linked turns. Remember to straighten your legs when the board turns downhill, then flex them again when you want to come back across the slope.'

Tom grinned. 'I'm bound to forget. I was terrible when I started skiing. I spent a whole week on the nursery slopes.' He laughed. 'Still, I got it in the end.'

'You did all right on the dry slope back home,' Lee said.

'It's different when you've got a teacher yelling out instructions.' Tom jumped his board round until it lay across the slope with the toe edge facing downhill. 'I hope I'm not going to make myself look a total idiot,' he said. 'Especially after that business with the drag-lift.'

They all laughed. Both boys had fallen off the drag-lift several times, much to the amusement of other people waiting in the queue. Manoeuvring a snowboard uphill was much more difficult than using a drag-lift while wearing skis. The noses of their boards kept digging into the snow.

'Don't remind me,' Lee said. He lifted his heels and let his snowboard slide across the slope. He shifted his weight on to his front foot. The board picked up speed. Lee let it run, relishing the soft 'swish' it made as it skimmed over the snow and the rush of cold air on his face. He was vaguely aware of a line of skiers zigzagging past on his right.

Lee reached the end of his first diagonal run. He leant back on his heels, slowing the board, ready to change direction and ride fakie, or backwards. As the snowboard came to a stop, he transferred his weight to his right leg and turned his shoulders towards the tail of his board. It moved back across the slope, edging downhill at a gentle angle. He leant forward and the board gathered speed again.

Lee's confidence grew. This was easier than he'd imagined it would be. The board moved so much more swiftly and lightly on snow.

Transferring his weight forward, Lee

steered round until he was facing downhill. The board accelerated, but as he attempted a toeside turn the tail came round too sharply, throwing him off balance. He fought to stay upright, but he could feel himself toppling backwards. In the end he landed on his back and began to skid down the slope. Quickly he jammed the edge of his board into the snow, stopping his slide.

Lee pushed himself upright again and looked around. Dominique was higher up the slope, leaning over. Beside her, Tom was sprawled on the snow. Lee smiled, relieved that he wasn't the only one falling over.

He tried another turn. This time, by letting the tail swing round more slowly, he managed to stay upright. Soon he was gliding across the slope, facing uphill. A surge of exhilaration swept through him. He'd done it!

Lee prepared to make a heelside turn. He fell over twice more before he reached the bottom of the hill, but his confidence was sky high. He was getting a feel for boarding on snow now and he was sure his next descent would be better.

He looked back. Tom was back on his feet. Lee was quite a way ahead of Tom and

Dominique. He watched them approach. Tom was moving fairly fast, grinning broadly. Dominique waved as she turned the nose of her board downhill and raced past Tom.

She stopped beside Lee. 'What did you think of it, then?' she asked.

'Fantastic!'

She smiled. 'Those turns you did looked pretty impressive. If I hadn't known this was your first time boarding on snow, I'd never have guessed.'

'I thought the way I fell over was best, though,' Lee laughed.

Tom reached them. 'That was brilliant!' There was snow on his woolly Bronx hat and inside the collar of his coat.

'How many times did you fall over?' Lee asked.

Tom shrugged. 'I lost count in the end. Let's get up to the top again and have another go.'

As they headed for the drag-lift, snow began to fall. Lee watched the dancing flakes delightedly. 'This'll be great for boarding on. Fresh snow's best.'

'As long as it doesn't snow *too* hard,'

Dominique warned them. 'The weather's very odd this year. We keep getting terrible blizzards.'

'It'll be all right,' Lee said. He didn't want to stop boarding now – not when he was just getting the hang of it. 'I've skied loads of times when it's been snowing.'

'But usually you know a storm will soon pass. This year, for some reason, a blizzard blows up very quickly, and it can last for hours.'

'We've got to have another run, though,' Lee said. 'We're only on the nursery slope after all. We can hardly get lost here. Even if there's a total white-out, we only need to head downhill and we'll come to the village.'

Dominique nodded. 'OK.'

The snow was falling hard by the time they reached the front of the drag-lift queue. Lee slipped the drag-lift button between his legs. This time, he held the nose of his board clear of the snow, determined not to repeat his earlier embarrassing falls.

When they reached the top of the slope, the snowflakes were whipping along almost horizontally, driven by an icy wind. Lee turned his collar up and pulled his hat down over his ears. He waited for Dominique and Tom to get off the drag-lift. 'Maybe this wasn't such a good idea after all,' he said, wiping snow from his goggles.

Dominique pointed to a square, flat-roofed café whose brightly lit windows shone out like a beacon through the whirling flakes. 'Let's have a hot drink while we wait and see if the snow stops.' They scooted across to it, took off their boards and went inside.

The café was half empty. They sat at a table near the window and watched the driving snow. Lee pulled off his gloves and warmed his fingers on his mug of hot chocolate. The only thing he could see outside was a thick, white, ever-moving curtain of snow.

They waited for nearly an hour, but the snow kept on falling. Gradually the café emptied until they were the only customers left. 'We might as well make a move,' Tom sighed. 'It's obvious we're not going to get back on the slopes today.' He sounded bitterly disappointed.

'Never mind,' Dominique said. 'The snow will be even better for snowboarding tomorrow.'

They paid their bill and went out into the driving snow to begin the long trudge on foot back to the village.

Lee stood on the chalet's doorstep, brushing the worst of the snow off his clothes. He took off his hat and shook it, sending the loose flakes twirling away on the wind. Then he pulled off his boots and went inside.

Jeff was sitting on the settee, watching television.

'There's a real blizzard blowing,' Lee said.

'Shhh,' Jeff said. 'I'm watching the news.'

'I didn't know you could speak French.'

'I can't. Not very well. That's why I need to concentrate.'

Lee glanced at the screen. A team of men and women were digging wearily through tonnes of snow. The camera panned round, showing a scene of total devastation: flattened buildings, overturned cars, trees snapped off.

'Was it an avalanche?' Tom asked, sinking into an armchair.

'Yes. Now be quiet, both of you.'

Lee stared at the images. Snow was falling thickly and the reporter's hair and clothes were covered in white flakes. Behind him, the rescuers were still working. The camera moved across the piled-up snow. Here and there, tree trunks or jagged, triangular roof timbers stuck up out of the snow. Lee could see a balcony rail, detached from its balcony but strangely undamaged.

At last the news item ended and Jeff switched the television off.

'Was it in France?' Tom asked. He sounded shocked.

Dominique nodded, her face grim. 'Only thirty kilometres from here. Five people dead and nine still missing. It knocked down many chalets.' She shook her head. 'You always think you're safe indoors.'

Tom shivered. Lee guessed he was thinking about the people who were missing. Maybe they were still alive under all that snow. Maybe they were lying there, listening to the sounds above them, willing the rescuers to reach them before their limited air supply ran out.

'It couldn't happen here, could it?' Tom asked. 'I mean, avalanches are pretty unusual …' He tailed off.

'Of course they're unusual,' Dominique said. 'The reporter said there's a big one like this once every hundred years. We should be

24

fine here, anyway. Our slopes aren't steep enough for a really big avalanche.'

Jeff stood up. 'There could be several smaller ones, though. It'll certainly stop skiers going off-piste – even with a guide – just to be on the safe side.' He went to the window and looked out.

'Hey, if the avalanche wasn't far away, maybe we should go and help,' Lee suggested excitedly.

'We can't get there,' Dominique said. 'The road's blocked. They're waiting for the weather to clear so they can fly in a mountain rescue team. But the forecast's for gale-force winds and blizzards right across the French Alps for the rest of tonight.'

Lee joined Jeff at the window. The snow was still coming down in bucketfuls and the wind was howling like a choir of mournful ghosts. He knew there were other chalets near by, but they were totally invisible. All he could see was swirling whiteness. He watched as the flakes touched the window pane.

'We'll phone home after dinner to let Mum and Dad know we're all right here,' Jeff said. 'You ought to phone your parents as well, Tom.' A bell rang in the kitchen. 'There's the timer. Dinner's ready. Can you two lay the table? The cutlery's in the drawer next to the cooker.'

They went into the kitchen. Jeff lifted the lid of a saucepan that was bubbling on top of the cooker, letting a cloud of evil-smelling steam escape. He stirred the contents vigorously. 'Perfect,' he said. 'Stew à la Jeff.'

Lee smiled grimly. 'Great, I can hardly wait.'

Jeff hurled a tea-towel at him. Lee ducked and grabbed a handful of knives and forks, and he and Tom retreated from the kitchen.

'Jeff's stew smells awful,' Tom said as they laid the table.

'If you think the smell's bad, wait till you taste it.' Lee laughed but Tom didn't join in. 'What's up?' Lee asked.

'I was thinking about that avalanche. What if one happens here? This chalet's just below the slopes. We'd be right in the firing-line.'

'The reporter said a big one like that only happens once every hundred years. And you heard Dominique: the slopes here aren't steep enough.'

'But suppose they're wrong.'

Jeff came in, carrying two steaming plates of stew.

'What's the point in worrying about an avalanche,' Lee whispered, 'when Jeff's about to poison us all?'

CHAPTER THREE

When Lee woke the next day, a pale, clear light was filtering through the curtains in the boys' bedroom. He clambered out of bed, shivering in the morning chill, and darted to the window. The snow had stopped falling. The sky was cornflower blue and the fresh snow sparkled in the sunshine as though it had been scattered with diamonds.

Tom rolled over in bed and yawned. 'Is it still snowing?'

'No. It's a brilliant day. Get up and let's go snowboarding.'

★

Jeff was gulping down coffee when the boys got downstairs. 'Sleep well?' he asked.

Lee rubbed his eyes. 'Like a log, bro.'

'I'm teaching this morning,' Jeff said, banging his empty mug down, 'so we'll go skiing this afternoon, yeah? I've hired you some skis.' He pulled on his boots. 'That's if the weather's OK. The forecast is for heavy snow and high winds.' He headed for the door. 'Don't go too far from the village, will you?'

The door slammed behind him.

'What a pain! He's obviously taken my mum's lecture on brotherly love a bit too literally,' Lee complained. 'I had hoped Dominique would give us another snow-boarding lesson this afternoon. I still want to learn how to do ollies.'

He hacked a chunk of French bread off the remains of the loaf they'd had with Jeff's stew the night before.

'I hope Jeff's not going to cook tonight,' Tom said, gulping down a glass of orange juice. 'I mean, it's nice of him to bother and all that … But those cafés in the high street look OK. We could try one of them.'

Lee pushed back his chair. 'Let's get a move

on,' he said. 'If it's going to snow like it did yesterday we ought to get out as soon as possible.'

Lee and Tom were on their way to the drag-lift when they saw a dark, stocky boy of about their own age coming out of a side street. He had a snowboard under his arm, with a picture of a moonlit mountain on it.

Lee stopped to get a better look. 'Your board's got brilliant graphics!' he called.

The boy came across to them, smiling. '*Merci*. I had it for Christmas.'

'Lucky thing.' Lee looked at his own board. It was red and black, with the occasional gold slash. He'd been pleased with it when he'd bought it but, compared to the French boy's board, it looked pretty ordinary. 'Does having a smart board improve your technique?' he asked, laughing.

The boy grinned. 'Perhaps. People expect you to be good, so you have to prove them right. Otherwise you look ...' He hesitated, evidently searching for the right word.

'A complete dork?' Lee suggested.

The boy's grin broadened.

'It wouldn't matter what sort of board I

had,' Tom said. 'I'd still manage to make myself look an idiot.'

They all laughed.

'Are you going to the halfpipe?' the boy asked.

'Halfpipe?' Lee stared at him. He hadn't realized there was a halfpipe at Chambeau.

'It is this way.' The boy pointed along the road. 'You want to come with me?'

'Yeah. How about it, Tom?'

Tom shrugged. 'What is it?'

'It's a sort of curved opening dug into the snow for freestylers to use,' Lee said. 'You know, one of those U-shaped things that snowboarders do jumps in.'

Tom nodded. 'Why not? But I'm only going to watch.'

They set off along the road.

'I'm Lee and this is Tom,' Lee said.

'My name is Marc. You have been in a halfpipe before?'

'No. But it'll be great to watch the experts.' Lee hoped to pick up some tips. It was through seeing a video of jumps – or airs, as snowboarders called them – that Lee had been inspired to take up the sport in the first place.

They had come to the edge of the village.

Below them, on the main road, a snowplough was crawling along, leaving a bank of snow at the roadside. 'Just over this hill,' Marc said, pointing ahead.

The snow lay in ridged furrows on the hillside. Deep footprint trails cut through it. From the top of the rise, a gentle slope led down to the halfpipe below. It was a wide channel dug into the snow. On either side, the snow was banked up high. There were about eight snowboarders using the halfpipe, zooming up the banks and jumping, sometimes falling in spectacular wipeouts. More people stood around watching, pointing out the more daring airs to their companions.

The three boys clipped on their leashes and strapped their snowboards on. Lee glanced at the freestylers in the halfpipe. Maybe, if he practised hard, before the week was out he'd be good enough to have a go at some of those airs.

'This afternoon I am going to the snowboard park in Val des Pins,' Marc said. 'Do you want to come?'

'What's it like?' Tom asked.

'Very fast, with many steep runs, banked turns and big hits. Also there are ramps.'

Lee's eyes lit up. 'It sounds brilliant!' Then he remembered Jeff's plans for the afternoon. 'But we've got to go skiing with my brother.' He sighed. A snowboard park would have been much more fun.

Tom snorted. 'We're hardly good enough for steep runs, banked turns and big hits,' he said. 'And imagine us two on ramps!'

'It'd be worth a visit, though,' Lee said. They could try the simpler bits of the course and learn how to handle the tricky areas by watching other snowboarders.

Tom laughed. 'I'm not going.'

Lee frowned. Tom could be a bit negative sometimes. 'We just need some more practice.' He turned to Marc. 'Where is this park?'

Marc fished a map out of his pocket. He pulled off his glove and pointed out the place. 'Here. Just outside Val des Pins, the next village. You can take the bus.' He pushed the map into Lee's hand. 'Keep it. I can get another from my hotel.'

Lee shoved the map into his pocket and zipped it up. He didn't want to lose it. He was going to try out the snowboard run before they reached the end of their holiday, whether Tom came with him or not.

'Now I am going back to the halfpipe,' Marc said. '*À bientôt*. See you later.'

Lee had been practising airs for about half an hour when it began to snow. He could clear the hit with ease now and he was trying to perfect an indy, by grabbing the toe edge of his board while he was in the air. Not that he'd had much success yet. He'd had a few embarrassing wipeouts, but he was persevering.

As the morning wore on, the falling snow worsened until it was hard for Lee to see where he was going. Twice he missed the hit altogether and rode on down the slope without jumping.

Tom came over from the halfpipe, where he'd been watching airs. 'The wind's getting up. Everyone's going. The halfpipe's deserted.'

Lee frowned. 'I was just about getting the hang of indys.'

Tom tutted and set off uphill. 'It's freezing. Let's go back to the chalet,' he called over his shoulder.

Lee took off his snowboard and ran after his friend. 'I'm with you there, mate. This snow'll turn into a blizzard in a minute.'

The snow whirled around them, driven by the icy wind, as they approached the top of the rise.

'I'll race you back to the village,' Tom said. 'You're on.'

They strapped their boards on and stood, side by side, at the top of the hill, peering into the whirling flakes. 'One, two, three, go!' Tom shouted.

They began to glide downhill. Lee was soon in front. He made steep turns, trying not to brake too hard. On the edge of the village he saw a heap of snow piled up. He was heading straight for it. Instinctively, he leant back on his heels, braking hard. But it was too late. There was no way he'd be able to stop in such a short distance. He prepared to jump.

He hit the bump at an awkward angle and soared into the air, fighting in vain to keep his balance. Crashing to the ground, he slid along on his back. Behind him, he heard Tom shout his name, but he couldn't stop: the snow was packed down hard here and he couldn't dig his snowboard in.

A shadowy group loomed up ahead. As he whizzed towards them, Lee saw that they were a party of skiers, returning from the slopes. Jeff was at the front of the group.

One of the skiers looked around. 'Watch out!' she called.

Horrified, Lee battled to steer round them. Jeff would go mad if he collided with a member of his skiing class.

They all leapt out of the way.

'Honestly, snowboarders are such a pain!' somebody complained in a loud voice as he whizzed by. Lee covered his face with his hands, hoping Jeff wouldn't recognize him. The movement sent his goggles flying, but he couldn't stop to pick them up.

He came to a halt at last and hurriedly unstrapped his feet. He looked around quickly. Jeff's skiing party was invisible behind the curtain of snow. There was no sign of Tom either. Lee picked up his snowboard and dashed home. Perhaps if he was sitting by the fire, reading, when Jeff came in, he might think Lee had been there all the time.

Letting himself into the chalet, he quickly brushed the snow off his snowboard and clothes, took off his boots and darted upstairs. In less than a minute he was downstairs again, with a book. He flopped into an armchair and opened the book. But he couldn't concentrate on reading. He was thinking about the snowboard course at Val des Pins – imagining the exhilaration of completing a run like that. He stared into the fire and smiled.

A few minutes later, Jeff came in. He stood in the open doorway for a few seconds, brushing the snow off his shoulders.

Lee looked up from his book, hoping that his face didn't show his guilt. 'Hi. How did your lessons go?'

'The lessons were fine.' Jeff took off his boots and left them by the door. 'It was when we got to the village that we met some trouble.' He came to the fire to warm his hands.

'This is a brilliant book,' Lee said. 'It's about …'

'A great, steaming idiot of a snowboarder nearly barged into my skiing party. Luckily somebody spotted him in time and shouted a warning, otherwise we'd probably have had some broken legs.'

'That's bad,' Lee said. 'Still, as long as nobody's hurt …'

Jeff fixed him with a hard stare. Lee looked

down at his book uncomfortably. He couldn't tell whether Jeff knew he was the runaway snowboarder or not.

'I believe these are yours,' Jeff snapped, tossing Lee his goggles.

'Sorry,' Lee said. 'There was this heap of snow, you see, and I …'

'I told you what I think of snowboarders. They don't give a moment's thought to anyone else.'

Tom came in. 'Lee, are you … ?' He broke off. 'Oh, hi, Jeff. It's snowing really hard out there. I don't reckon we'll get any skiing in this afternoon.'

'We'll all have to stay in together,' Jeff said. 'Won't that be fun?' He made it sound like a threat.

Lee stood up. 'I've just remembered something I've got to do in my bedroom.' He headed for the stairs.

Tom came after him.

'That snowboarding run at Val des Pins sounds brilliant,' Lee said when they were safely in their room.

Tom pulled a face. 'We're not ready for it. It'd be better to wait until the end of the week when we've had more practice.'

'But we'll learn new techniques from watching other snowboarders.'

Tom eyed him suspiciously. 'You just want to go and watch?'

'Mostly. Though we could try out the easy bits of the course while we're there.'

'If there are any.'

'Shall we go tomorrow then?' Lee enthused.

'I don't know. Let's have a look at the leaflet Marc gave you.'

Lee stood up. 'It's in my coat. I'll nip down and get it.'

He was back in no time. 'Here. It's written in English on the back.' They pored over the leaflet. The pictures showed people performing breath-taking airs and skilful carved turns. 'It says here that some areas of the course are simpler than others,' Lee said. 'So that settles it, we should go.'

Tom laughed. 'All right. I can see you're not going to shut up until I give in. But if you break your leg or something, don't expect any sympathy from me.'

CHAPTER FOUR

The snow lay in thick pleats round the chalet when Tom and Lee got up next morning. 'I've never seen anything like this,' Lee said, surveying the deep, unsullied whiteness.

They dressed hurriedly, then went out on to the balcony. The sun was out and the sky was clear and blue. Across the road, a man was standing on a chalet roof, shovelling snow into the garden below. When he straightened up, they could see that the snow reached to his chest.

'I suppose he's clearing it so it doesn't fall on anyone,' Tom said.

Lee's eyes lit up. 'I wonder if Jeff wants us to climb up and clear our roof.'

'No, I don't,' Jeff called from the landing. 'You'd probably fall off and break your necks.' He came into their bedroom. 'Not that I'd mind *you* breaking *your* neck, little brother,' he said, with a wicked grin, 'but Mum would probably give me a hard time over it.' He spotted Lee's jester hat and tutted.

Tom and Lee came back into the bedroom and shut the balcony door.

'What are your plans for today?' Jeff asked. 'The lower slopes are still open, but the high ones have been closed because of the avalanche risk.'

Lee tried to look innocent; he knew Jeff would disapprove of them going to the snowboard park. 'We're not quite sure. Will you be teaching?'

'Yes. I'll be back late afternoon.'

Lee flashed Tom a quick smile. Jeff wouldn't be able to stop them from going to Val des Pins if he was out of the way.

'You look very shifty, Lee,' Jeff said suspiciously. 'What are you up to?'

'Nothing.'

Jeff's eyes narrowed. 'You're not planning anything stupid, are you?'

'No. How could you suggest such a thing? I never do anything stupid.'

Jeff gave a mocking laugh and turned to go, but then he stopped and picked up the leaflet about the snowboard park. Lee's heart sank. He should never have left it out. 'You're not planning to go here, are you?' Jeff wanted to know.

Lee shrugged.

'It's a course for experts.'

'Some parts are easier,' Lee said defensively. 'And you don't have to complete the whole thing.'

Jeff sighed heavily. 'Look at the weather. How are you going to get there?'

'By bus.'

'And suppose there's another blizzard while you're there? How will you get home?'

Lee glowered at him. Sometimes Jeff didn't seem to realize that he wasn't a kid any more! 'We're not idiots, you know. We won't go if the weather looks bad. And if it starts clouding over, we'll come straight home. The snowploughs'll keep the road open.'

Jeff turned to Tom. 'Don't let him talk you into doing anything dangerous.'

'I won't. We'll be fine.'

Jeff glanced at his watch. 'I've got to go. But mind you keep an eye on the weather.'

Lee waited until he heard the front door slam, then he tossed a few things into his backpack: the map, some bottled water, a bar of chocolate, a first-aid kit, a whistle, his wallet, some board wax, and his tool kit, so that he would be able to adjust the bindings on his board. He slung the bag over his shoulder and hurried downstairs. 'We ought to get a move on, just in case it does snow again later.'

Tom followed more slowly. 'You did mean what you said, didn't you? We will come home if the weather looks bad.'

'Of course.' Lee pulled on his coat and boots. 'Now come on.'

Marc was waiting at the bus-stop. 'Hello,' he said, grinning. 'Are you going to Val des Pins?'

Lee smiled back. 'That's right. You?'

Marc nodded. 'The weather was not good yesterday, so I am going today instead.'

Lee's smile widened. He'd be able to pick

up lots of tips from Marc. 'It looks as though it'll be sunny all day today,' he said, glancing up at the cloudless sky.

The bus soon arrived and the boys piled on, in high spirits. The sun streamed in through the windows, making it hot inside. They sat at the back, on the long seat, with Lee in the middle, and leant their snowboards against the window. Lee took his coat off and laid it over the back of the seat in front of him. There were only three other passengers: two young women holiday reps, wearing distinctive scarlet coats, and a bearded man in his forties.

As Lee had predicted, the road was clear and they made good time. It was only a quarter past ten when they saw the village of Val des Pins ahead. Further off, on the far side of the valley, stood the forest of pine trees that gave the village its name, *Valley of the Pines*.

Lee pulled out his map. 'According to this, the snowboard course should be on our left.' He looked up, trying to spot it.

'*Voilà!* There,' Marc said, pointing uphill. A couple of snowboarders were snaking down the mountainside. Lee drew in his breath sharply. Even from this distance he could tell that they were moving at an incredible speed. A thrill of excitement ran down his spine. He watched eagerly as the front snowboarder swerved round a sharp bend, then took off from a ramp. He soared into the air and bent forward to grab the edge of his board. Then he flipped over and made a perfect landing, before racing on down the mountain.

'I hope you don't expect me to do that,' Tom said, laughing.

'Not just yet,' Lee joked. But perhaps, he thought, if they practised hard all week, they'd be good enough to attempt a less tricky jump from the ramp before they had to fly back to England.

The road ahead curved sharply. The driver slowed down. Then, as they turned the corner, they saw that a lorry had stopped, directly in their path.

Lee gasped.

The driver braked hard, throwing the passengers forward, but it was clear the bus wouldn't be able to stop in time. The driver hauled on the wheel and the bus slewed round. Now it was heading for a wall of rock at the edge of the road.

'Hang on!' Lee cried, bracing himself for the

impact. The bus hit the rocks with a violent jolt that sent Lee sprawling into the aisle. Tom and Marc were thrown forward against the backs of the seats in front of them. There was a deafening crash and sparks flew as rock tore into metal. One of the holiday reps screamed. The bus rocked wildly, then veered back across the road. Finally, it juddered to a halt.

'*Ça va, tout le monde?* Is everyone all right?' the driver cried.

Lee sat up shakily, carefully brushing small pieces of glass from his hair.

'Are you OK?' Tom asked. He held out his hand to Lee, to help him up.

'Yeah.' Lee could feel a slight bump on the side of his head, but it was nothing worth worrying about. 'What about you two?'

'Yeah. Just a bit shaken up,' Tom said.

'OK,' Marc said.

Lee looked around as he got to his feet. The holiday reps and the man with the beard looked deathly white, but they didn't appear to be hurt either. Two windows on the left side of the bus were smashed. Several empty seats were littered with glass. 'Lucky there were hardly any passengers,' he said, sinking back into his seat.

'The lorry driver was an imbecile to stop there,' Marc said angrily. 'We could all have been killed.' He picked up the snowboards, which had slid halfway under the seat in front. 'I hope these are OK.'

They examined their boards carefully, but there seemed to be no damage. 'That's a relief, then,' Tom said. 'I don't know what we'd have done if they'd got broken.'

Lee balanced his board against the back of the seat and stood up again. 'I'm going outside for some fresh air.' His knees were still shaking from the crash and he hoped that a short walk might calm his nerves.

The bus door stood open. Lee stepped down on to the road. He heard angry voices coming from the far side of the bus and moved towards them. The driver was arguing with a chubby man dressed in blue overalls.

Tom and Marc joined him. 'What are they saying?' Tom asked Marc.

'The lorry driver says his lorry has broken down,' Marc translated. 'He thinks the bus driver was going too fast.'

'Look at the state of the bus,' Lee said, pointing. The front was staved in and one wheel was hopelessly buckled. The left side, that had borne the brunt of the impact, was misshapen and a long, jagged gash had opened up in the metal. It was clear the bus was past being driven.

At last the bus driver turned away from the lorry driver with an angry snort. '*Montez, s'il vous plaît.* Go inside, please,' he said, ushering the boys back on board. While they were finding their way back to their seats, the driver made a call on a mobile phone.

'Surely the bus is too badly damaged to go on,' Tom said.

'Perhaps they'll bring another bus out here,' Lee suggested. 'I hope they hurry up, though.' He was feeling better now and was keen to get to the snowboard park.

The driver put his phone back in his pocket and turned to face the passengers. 'My English is not good,' he said apologetically. 'Is there someone who can translate for me?'

'I will,' one of the holiday reps said. She moved to the front of the bus.

The driver began to speak in French. 'He's very sorry about the accident,' the rep translated. 'The bus can't go any further. His company are sending a replacement from

Chambeau but it'll take about half an hour to get here, and it can't take us on to Val des Pins because the bus and lorry are blocking the road. Apparently a breakdown truck will come from Val Thorens, but it won't be here for quite a while.'

Lee groaned. 'What a pain!' He slumped back in his seat. 'We might as well have stayed in Chambeau.'

'Never mind,' Tom said. 'The snowboard course looks impossibly difficult anyway.'

Lee glanced up at it. 'We're pretty close to it here. We could walk it easily.'

Marc shook his head. 'It is uphill all the way.'

'We're closer to the village,' Tom said. 'Why don't we walk down there and get the cable car? Look, you can see one now. It goes straight to the park.'

'A good idea,' Marc agreed.

Lee shook his head. 'It'll take longer – and anyway there'll be a massive queue. Walking from here will be better.' He caught Tom's hand and pulled him up. 'Come on.'

'Not me,' Marc said. 'I prefer the easy life. I will take the cable car from the village and meet you at the park.'

'How will we get back to Chambeau, later?' Tom asked uneasily.

'The road's bound to be cleared before long, so we can get the cable car to Val des Pins and catch a bus from there.' Lee picked up his snowboard and made for the door, crunching over broken glass. 'Come on. Let's get going.'

Tom and Marc followed him. 'OK. But I think you're mad,' Tom said. 'I'd much rather go in the cable car.'

Lee looked up at the sky as he got off the bus. He'd promised Jeff that they wouldn't go if the weather looked bad, but the sky was bright blue and cloudless. 'It looks as though the weather's going to be OK,' he said, glancing at Tom and Marc. 'What do you think?'

Marc nodded. 'It is very sunny. No snow today, I think.' He set off along the road in the direction of the village. 'I will see you at the top,' he called.

'We'll be there first,' Lee called back as he and Tom set off up the mountain.

CHAPTER FIVE

It was much harder reaching the snowboard park than it had looked from the road. Lee and Tom had to keep making long detours round unclimbable cliffs, and they sank into the snow at every step. 'This is going to take ages,' Tom complained breathlessly when they'd been walking for about half an hour. 'We should have gone down to the village with Marc and caught the cable car.'

Lee stopped for a breather. He was hot from the exertion of climbing, so he unzipped his coat and stuffed his hat in his pocket. Then he turned and looked back down the mountainside. The bus was a long way below. The driver, his dark uniform clearly visible, was pacing up and down.

'Come on, Tom,' Lee said. 'We'll never get to the park at this rate.' He set off again, heading in the direction of the cable car station. Tom trailed after him.

At last Lee stopped again. 'There's a bit of a dip here,' he called excitedly, surveying the series of small, undulating dips and rises ahead. 'We can snowboard for quite a way.'

Tom nodded approvingly and strapped on his board. 'This looks great. Just what we need after that climb.'

'If we get up enough speed we should be able to keep going on the next uphill section,' Lee said. 'And we can probably manage a few jumps, too.'

'Race you to the other side,' Tom said, launching himself down the slope.

'Bet I win!' Lee took off after him. He kept the nose of his board facing downhill for most of the run, so that it would travel swiftly. Tom was moving more cautiously, taking a diagonal line, and Lee soon overtook him.

The run was exhilarating. Lee used all his

skills to stay upright, leaning into curves and using his arms to balance himself. Twice he jumped at the top of a small rise, before sweeping on. At last he reached a steep upward slope. He cruised up for a few metres before stopping, then dug the heel edge of his board into the snow so he wouldn't slide down.

Tom was not too far behind. 'Hurry up,' Lee called. 'I've been here for ages.'

Tom stopped just below him. 'Rubbish! I almost caught you.'

Lee looked up the mountain, hoping to see the cable car terminus. Dark clouds were building up overhead. 'Oh no! Look at the sky,' he said.

Tom frowned uneasily. 'It looks as though we're in for a really bad snowfall after all.' He looked back down the mountain. 'Perhaps we should go back to the bus.'

Lee glanced at his watch. They'd been climbing for nearly an hour. 'The replacement bus will be long gone before we get there,' he pointed out. 'Then we'll have to walk all the way into Val des Pins.'

'It'll probably be best to go on to the cable car station, then,' Tom said. 'We can ride down to the village from there if the weather's bad.'

They went on, climbing as quickly as they could, though the deep snow slowed their progress.

Suddenly, Tom plunged into a snowdrift. His snowboard slipped from his grasp. Lee lunged at it, desperately trying to catch it. He was too slow. The board slid away down the mountainside. Tom struggled out of the drift. 'I've got to get it back!' he cried. 'My dad'll go mad if I lose it.' He began to run downhill, floundering through the powdery snow.

'I'll get it,' Lee said. He hurriedly fastened on his own snowboard and set off after it. The ground was steep here, much steeper than any slope Lee had boarded on before. He knew he'd have to move down in carved turns and he'd got to get them right. If he went too slowly, he'd lose Tom's board – it was zooming away at an alarming speed. But if he tried to go too quickly, he'd fall over. The gradient was so steep, he wasn't sure he'd be able to stop himself if that happened.

'Be careful!' Tom called out, as Lee sped away.

Lee concentrated on the terrain ahead, trying to steer a course over the smoothest ground and around rocks. His heart was pounding as he swooped down the slope, but he was also exhilarated. There was something fantastically exciting about being off-piste, about having to rely on your instincts to stay upright. Now he could see why free-riding was so popular.

The wind stung Lee's face, but he barely noticed it. He was too busy concentrating on changing from the heelside to the toeside edge of his board as he carved his way downhill. Tom's board was running on ahead of him, a streak of bright blue against the brilliant white snow.

Suddenly Lee saw a broad ridge ahead of him. He was coming out of a heelside carve and he eased the nose of his board round and ran on across the slope, parallel to the ridge. He didn't want to jump if he could avoid it – he wasn't skilful enough yet to guarantee that he'd land properly. But the ridge stretched on for as far as he could see, and he was moving further and further away from the fall line of Tom's board.

'I'll have to jump,' he said out loud, trying

to convince himself. He rotated his shoulders and rolled the board on to the toe edge so it began to turn. The nose came round until it was pointing downhill. The board gathered speed. Lee drew in his breath sharply as it flew towards the ridge. He soared off the top.

For a moment, he seemed to hang in the air.

Then he hit the ground.

His board began to tilt. He flung out his arms, struggling to keep his balance. For a few agonizing seconds he thought he was going to fall and go plunging down the mountainside, but at last he managed to regain control. Slowing down, he looked about him for Tom's board. It was quite a way below him, sliding towards a snow-covered bush.

Lee rode after it. By the time he reached the bush, the board had stopped. Its leash was entangled in the branches. Lee sat down beside it. As he released his feet, he looked back up the mountain. Tom was a long way above him. Lee smiled with satisfaction: he'd covered a fair distance and he hadn't fallen over once. His smile soon faded, though, at the thought of the long walk uphill that lay ahead of him.

He pulled Tom's board out of the bush and examined it. There were a couple of shallow scrapes on the bottom and the tail was a bit chipped, but the damage didn't look too serious. He held the board up above his head to signal to Tom that it was OK.

Tom waved and gave him the thumbs-up sign. Lee tucked both boards under his arm and began the long trudge uphill.

He hadn't gone far before the snow began to fall lightly. He squinted up the mountain, searching for Tom, trying to mark the direction he needed to take in case it started snowing harder and obscured his view. Tom was moving cautiously down the slope towards him.

Lee went on, but soon the snow was falling harder and the wind began to rise. It hurled the flakes this way and that, creating a moving, lacy curtain that suddenly hid Tom from Lee's sight. 'I know the direction to take, though,' Lee said, trying to reassure himself. He gulped down the knot of anxiety that had risen in his throat. All he had to do was stick to the line he was on and he'd soon meet up with Tom.

But keeping in a straight line was almost impossible when you were walking blind through deep snow and carrying two snowboards. Lee desperately wanted to shout out Tom's name. If his friend heard him and called back, Lee could follow the sound of his voice. But he knew this was too dangerous. He was moving through newly fallen snow on a steep slope – any sudden loud noise could trigger an avalanche on terrain like this. He shuddered, remembering the pictures he'd seen on the television news.

Pushing the images to the back of his mind, he pressed on. The snow was falling harder, stinging his face. Up and up. Up and up. Lee was panting hard and his knees ached painfully, but he didn't dare stop for a rest. He had to keep going: he'd got to find Tom.

His head began to be filled with doubts. What if he couldn't find Tom? What if he passed by him and went on up the mountain? Even though it was broad daylight, he didn't like the idea of himself and Tom being separated out here on this lonely mountain.

Lee wiped snow from his goggles and kept climbing, wishing he'd never suggested walking to the snowboard park. He tried to be positive, to remind himself that every step he took brought him closer to his friend. Once they were back together, they could search for the cable car station. Lee thought longingly of the mountainside restaurant they'd find there. Sipping scalding-hot chocolate by a roaring fire would be heaven after this.

The wind dropped for a moment. Lee squinted ahead, trying to make out some familiar object that would tell him whether he was on course. And then he saw it. A dark shape – a human shape. Hope swelled inside him. Surely it must be Tom. Nobody else would be wandering around on the mountainside in this weather.

Lee headed towards the figure, his flagging energy miraculously boosted. The wind picked up again, blocking his view, but Lee knew where he was going now. As he drew near, he called softly: 'Tom, is that you?'

'Lee. Thank God!'

Lee ran the last few steps. Tom was standing in the shelter of a rocky cliff. He looked frozen.

Lee's face broke into a broad grin. 'I was worried I'd pass you without noticing.'

'Same here. I've been wandering around looking for you for ages.'

'We'd better get a move on,' Lee said. 'I could murder a hot drink.'

They set off once again up the mountain. 'Do you think we'll be able to find the cable car station?' Tom asked. 'I mean, you can hardly see a thing now. This snowstorm's turning into another blizzard, I reckon.'

His words echoed Lee's own worries, but Lee shrugged off his doubts. 'We managed to find each other, didn't we? Tracking down something as big as a cable car station should be a doddle.'

But it wasn't a doddle. On and on they trudged, climbing all the time, peering blindly into the snowstorm. Now and then rocky outcrops blocked their path and they would have to make a long detour to get round them.

At last Tom stopped. 'I reckon we've come too far,' he said. 'We must have missed it.'

Lee came to a halt beside him. They seemed to have been climbing for ages. He peeled back the cuff of his glove and looked at his watch. 'It's half past two,' he said in disbelief. They'd left the bus over three hours before.

'I knew it,' Tom moaned. 'We've gone too far.' He slumped down in the snow.

Lee sat beside him, glad of the chance to rest his aching legs.

'What are we going to do?' Tom asked, sounding as if he was beginning to panic.

'We'll be OK.' Lee tried to think logically. There was no reason to get hysterical, even if they had missed the cable car terminus. True they were halfway up an unfamiliar mountain in the middle of a snowstorm. But it was still only mid-afternoon, so there'd be a couple of hours of daylight left yet. Surely they couldn't be in any danger.

'We don't even know which direction to take,' Tom said.

'Perhaps it'd be better to go back to the road,' Lee suggested. 'Then we can walk on to the village or sit in the broken-down bus, depending on how bad the weather is.'

'How shall we find the road again? We can hardly see a thing.'

'Keep heading downhill. We're bound to reach it eventually.' Lee opened his backpack and pulled out the water bottle and a bar of chocolate. He gave half of the chocolate to Tom. 'Here. Eat this, then we'll get going again.'

They ate the chocolate and swigged down the water in silence.

Finally Lee stood up. 'Let's go,' he said, trying to think of a way to lighten the gloomy mood that had settled on them. 'It'll be easier now. It's downhill all the way.'

CHAPTER SIX

They had been walking for about twenty minutes when the snow eased off a little. 'This is more like it,' Lee said. 'We'll be able to see where we're going now.' He strapped on his snowboard.

'You're not planning to ride down, are you?' Tom demanded.

'It beats walking, and it'll be much quicker.'

'But it's so steep in places.'

'We can sideslip or even climb down the worst bits and board the rest of the way.'

Tom pursed his lips. 'And suppose we fall?'

'We'll go slowly. Don't worry, we'll be all right.' Lee had had enough of walking. The snow was so soft that their feet sank in at every step. Lifting them clear was exhausting. Besides, he wanted to get off the mountain as quickly as possible in case the weather became worse.

'I'm not riding,' Tom said.

'Don't be an idiot.' Lee was becoming exasperated. 'We'll get down much faster if we board. For a start, we'll skim over the top of the snow instead of sinking into it.'

'It's not me who's being an idiot,' Tom snapped. 'You know I can't board as well as you. It'll be fine for you, but I'll keep falling over all the time. Most likely I'll go skidding over some cliff.' His face was white, and Lee realized that he was really scared.

'Listen, you can set the pace. I'll go as slow as you like. And we can take our boards off when we get to a tricky bit.'

Tom's scowl lifted a little.

'I mean, this bit in front of us looks OK, doesn't it?' Lee went on. The slope was fairly gentle with hardly any undulations. 'It's not much steeper than a nursery slope.'

Tom nodded. 'Well, yes …'

'So we might as well board down it.'

'Just this bit, then. But that doesn't mean I'm boarding all the way to the road.'

'OK.' Lee stood up. He jumped his board round and waited impatiently while Tom fastened his own bindings. 'Let's go, then,' he said when Tom was ready. He pulled his friend up. 'Do you want to go in front?'

Tom shook his head. 'You go first. But don't go too fast.'

Lee let his board run diagonally across the slope, setting an easy course that he knew Tom could follow and braking hard if he thought his friend was falling behind.

Gradually the slope became steeper. Rocks protruded from the snow here and there. Lee glanced back, wondering if he should stop. But Tom seemed to be doing fine. He was close behind Lee, leaning into the turns like a true professional and steering easily round the rocks. 'How are you doing?' Lee called over his shoulder.

'OK.'

Lee kept going, glad that they were making such good time. At this rate, they'd be off the mountain long before it grew dark. The thought encouraged him. Maybe they'd even manage to get back to Chambeau before Jeff came in. That way he'd never find out what a disastrous day they'd had.

All at once, Lee's board shuddered – he'd clipped a rock concealed under the snow. He fought to stay upright, flinging out his arms and leaning forward, but he was thrown over. He somersaulted twice, then went skidding downhill on his front. Struggling to stop his slide, he dug the toe edge of his board in and clawed frantically at the snow with his hands.

He heard Tom calling his name but there was no time to reply. He had to concentrate all his efforts on stopping. He knew the dangers of being off-piste. There could be anything ahead of him: a wall of rock, a tree – or worse – a precipice.

Lee's board hit another rock and bounced off, jolting him painfully. A moment later the snow under him gave way. He plunged downwards, scrabbling vainly for a handhold, desperate to stop his fall – terrified that he'd plunged into a deep crevice and that the bottom could be hundreds of metres below.

Suddenly his knees hit something hard and he jerked to a stop. He cleared the snow from his face and then lay still, gasping for breath. He ached all over and his heart was racing furiously. He opened his eyes wide and lifted his head, trying to see where he was, but the blue-tinged gloom only showed him that he was buried in snow. And he knew the danger wasn't over yet. If he *was* in a crevice, he might have landed on a narrow ledge. The slightest movement could send him plummeting to his death.

But he couldn't stay here for ever. He was totally covered – obviously the snow he'd dislodged as he fell had caved in on top of him – so Tom might not be able to find him. Lee took a deep, steadying breath. If he was going to get out of here, it was up to him to do something.

Slowly, cautiously, he removed his glove and reached down to feel the surface that had broken his fall. If it was grass, then he was in a snowdrift. If it was rock, then there was a fair chance he'd plunged into a crack in the ground.

'Let it be grass,' he prayed. His fingers touched something hard and spiky. He pushed further down. The spiky objects bent aside and he found a hard, solid surface. His hopes soared. The spiky things were blades of grass, frozen stiff! Grass! He'd fallen into a snowdrift!

Weak with relief, he got to his knees. Turning awkwardly, he released his feet from his snowboard and stood up. His head broke through the surface of the snow. He looked around.

He was at the side of a wide, high, craggy rock. The drift had built up against it; the snow lay, shoulder-deep, in a graceful curve, sculpted by the wind. Tom was standing a little way off, further up the slope, his face pale and drawn. 'Lee! Are you all right?' he cried.

'I will be when I get out of this drift.' Lee reached out across the snow in an attempt to find something to get hold of. However, his arms simply sank into the snow.

'I'll pull you out,' Tom said.

'Don't come too close,' Lee warned. 'It'll make things twice as bad if you fall in, too.' He spotted his hat lying near by, half-buried in the snow. He picked it up, shook the snow out of it and put it on. It felt cold and wet.

Tom lay down on the snow, spreading his weight so he wouldn't sink too far. He inched forward on his stomach and reached out a hand to Lee.

'Hang on. Take my snowboard first.' Lee extracted it from the drift and slid it across to his friend.

'Grab the back binding,' Tom said. 'I'll pull you out with it.'

Lee pushed his fingers into the binding. Tom caught hold of the front one and wriggled backwards, pulling the board with him. Lee felt himself move a fraction. He kicked hard, trying to work his way out of the drift. Soon he was lying, flat out, on top of the snow. He rested for a moment, panting from the exertion.

'Get a move on,' Tom said.

Lee wriggled, snakelike, towards him and stood up gingerly, hoping he was clear of the drift. He sank to his knees. 'That's better,' he said. Shivering, he scooped snow out of the neck of his jacket. 'I'm freezing,' he complained. 'Let's hope it's not too far to go now. I'm dying for a hot drink.' He sat down and scraped the snow out of the bindings on his snowboard.

'What are you doing?' Tom asked sharply.

'I can't get my feet in if the bindings are full of snow.'

'You're not going to ride again! You were lucky to fall in a drift before, but you could just as easily have gone over a cliff.'

'I clipped that rock because I wasn't

looking properly,' Lee said. 'I'll give any suspicious-looking bumps a wide berth from now on.'

'Well, I'm not boarding any more,' Tom said firmly.

Lee turned to look down the mountain. He wanted to know how much further they'd have to go before they reached the road. He was beginning to feel uneasy about the time it was taking them. He didn't fancy being out on the mountain in the dark. The snow was still falling and he couldn't see that far ahead. He looked at his watch. It was nearly four o'clock. 'It'll be dark soon,' he said. 'We've got to get down quickly.'

'Come on then,' Tom said. He began to walk down the mountainside, his back stiff with determination.

Lee followed him. 'Go on, Tom. Snowboarding'll get us down faster.'

'No.' Tom kept walking.

'Tom.'

'I said no.'

The snow fell more thickly, closing in around them so that they were cut off from their surroundings. Lee fell silent. Tom was right, there was no way they could snowboard in weather like this.

It was getting dark, the snowstorm was rapidly becoming a blizzard, and the boys still hadn't found the road. They trudged on, heads down, too exhausted to talk.

Suddenly Lee stopped. The ground ahead ended abruptly. Tom came alongside him and Lee put out an arm to prevent him from going too close to the edge.

'What's up?' Tom had to shout to make his voice heard above the howling wind.

'We're on the edge of a cliff, I think.' Lee crouched down and squinted. The ground fell away steeply. He shivered. If he hadn't noticed it, they'd have plunged over. He strained his eyes into the whirl of blinding snow but he couldn't see the bottom of the drop: it could be one metre or one hundred metres below.

'What are we going to do?' Tom asked despairingly.

'We'll have to go back.' Lee's heart sank at the thought. Despite their weariness, they'd have to climb back up this steep slope and find another way down. 'We'll have to be careful, too,' he added. If they slipped while they were above this precipice, they'd slide straight over the edge.

'We're lost, aren't we?' Tom said, his voice sharp with fear, as they began to make their way uphill again.

Lee swallowed the hard lump that had risen in his throat. For an hour or more now he'd known that they were lost, but hearing it put into words brought home the dangerous reality of their situation. They were lost on a mountainside, battling through a blizzard, with night coming on fast.

His stomach churned at the thought. In situations like this, people died. Overcome with weariness, they lay down in the snow and froze to death. *But that's not going to happen to us*, he thought fiercely, fighting down his own fear. He and Tom were going to keep battling until they reached safety. They'd never give in.

'Which way now?' Tom asked. They'd reached a rocky outcrop that blocked their path.

Lee shrugged. It really didn't matter whether they turned left or right; they had no way of knowing where either direction would lead them. 'Let's go left,' he suggested, ignoring the inner voice that wouldn't let him forget that this was all his fault. They turned left and clambered slowly and carefully along the edge of the rock, still holding on tightly to their snowboards.

By the time they reached the place where the rock petered out, the snow had eased a little. 'Things'll be better now,' Lee said, trying to lift their spirits. 'We'll be able to go a bit faster.'

'Shall we try heading downhill again?' Tom suggested.

'Definitely. The road might be just below us now.'

The ground sloped steeply downhill, but they couldn't see whether it led to the road or not. Lee knew that they could easily start an avalanche on a slope like this, but they'd have to take that risk. They'd got to get off the mountain by the fastest route possible, before the light faded altogether.

They started down the slope, leaning back and moving cautiously so that they wouldn't fall. They were walking into the wind now, and the snow whipped their faces and clung to their eyelashes, making their eyes feel heavy. Lee fought the urge to shut his eyes and sleep.

He was tired, so tired … It would be such a relief to lie down and rest …

Tom's hand on his arm jerked him back to reality. 'It's getting steeper, Lee. We ought to cross the slope diagonally or we'll fall.'

'OK.' They turned wearily and trudged on, hauling each foot through the powdery snow, with Tom slightly ahead.

Suddenly, without warning, Tom tripped over a hidden rock and fell forward with a gasp of pain. His snowboard slipped from his grasp and skidded away down the slope.

Before Lee could reach him, Tom himself began to roll down the mountainside. 'Lee! Help!' he shrieked.

Lee's heart leapt into his mouth. It was impossible to tell what lay at the bottom of the slope. He had to catch his friend and stop his fall. But he'd never do it on foot and, if he tried to run, he'd surely fall. He threw his board down, pushed his feet into the bindings and fastened them hurriedly. There wasn't time to strap the leash to his leg, so he tucked it into his boot to stop it trailing.

Then he was off. He couldn't see Tom, but he was able to follow the trail of churned-up snow he'd left. Lee raced on, his heart hammering, keeping the nose of his snowboard pointing as far downhill as he dared so he could go as quickly as possible. He was flashing along, riding faster and faster. Sweat trickled down his back and his hands felt clammy inside his gloves. He leant over, to the side, backwards, forwards, twisting his upper body, crouching low, speeding in and out of steep turns.

And now he was catching up. He could just make Tom out in the twilight. He'd stopped rolling, but he was still sliding at full tilt, his arms and legs working frantically as he tried to bring himself to a halt.

Lee pushed himself harder and drew closer to his friend. He reached out, bracing himself. He mustn't let Tom pull him off-balance.

'Give me your hand, Tom.'

Tom stuck out a hand. Lee caught it. He leant back hard, battling to keep his balance, braking furiously.

The snowboard slowed. Lee was winning the fight. They were travelling much less quickly now. If he could just bring the nose of his board round, across the slope, he could probably stop their slide altogether.

He looked ahead and his blood ran cold.

Just a few metres in front of them, the slope came to an end – in a vertical drop.

Tom gave a sudden desperate cry: 'My glove!' A moment later, he slid away from Lee, leaving his empty glove in Lee's hand. Lee toppled backwards and began to slide downhill. He rammed the heel edge of his board hard into the snow and skidded to a stop.

But there was nothing he could do for Tom. His friend was now at the bottom of the slope.

A moment later, with a shriek of terror, he plunged over the edge.

CHAPTER SEVEN

Lee couldn't move. He was turned to stone by the horror of Tom's fall. He stared at the cliff edge, wide-eyed, his mind numbed by shock.

Tears began to fill his eyes, but he blinked them away angrily. Crying wouldn't help. Trembling, he rolled over and heaved himself upright. Then he sideslipped down the mountainside on shaking legs, terrified by what he might see.

He reached the edge of the drop and looked over. Tom was lying on his back in the snow, about four metres below. He wasn't moving.

'Tom!' Lee yelled desperately, no longer caring about the risk of starting an avalanche. 'Tom, are you all right?' He released his feet hurriedly and let his snowboard drop over the edge, not caring what happened to it. Reaching Tom was all that mattered.

There was no easy way down. Lee was standing on the edge of a sheer drop with no jutting ledges to help him climb down. And the cliff was wide, stretching out to left and right for as far as he could see. He ran to his right, searching frantically. No way down in that direction!

He turned and pelted back, pausing briefly to glance down at his friend as he passed above him. Tom still hadn't moved. Lee ran to his left, praying that he'd find a way to reach Tom. On and on he ran. But the cliff rose higher, making the drop longer. Eventually he turned back, knowing it was hopeless.

Tom still hadn't moved, and Lee could see, even from this height, that the snow was settling on him, turning his clothes white. Lee's stomach turned over. He'd got to get down there. Tom could die of hypothermia if he was left alone in the freezing snow for too long.

If he isn't dead already, Lee thought grimly.

He sat on the edge of the cliff and let his feet dangle over. Mustering all his courage, he prepared to jump down. It was his only chance of reaching Tom. But his friend was an alarmingly long way down. If Lee landed awkwardly, he could break a leg. He guessed they'd both die if that happened. Lying out in the open, unable to move …

Lee swallowed his fear. He took a deep breath, shut his eyes and launched himself off the cliff. It felt as though he was falling for ages, though it must have been less than a second before he hit the snow below. He rolled over, then stood up, filled with sudden, overwhelming relief that he was all right. He ran to his friend.

'Tom!'

Tom's hat and goggles had come off and he was crying, his eyes screwed up with pain. A long gash above Tom's left eyebrow made Lee jump back in fright. Blood was oozing out and trickling down Tom's face. The snow to one side of his head was stained red.

'Oh no! No!' Panic boiled up inside Lee. He fought it down frantically. Feverishly he pulled off his backpack, rummaged inside and found his first-aid kit. Yanking off his gloves, he wrenched open the small tin box, grateful now that his mother had insisted on him bringing it. There wasn't much inside: a pack of plasters, a bandage, a roll of gauze, some safety pins, folding scissors and a miniature tube of antiseptic cream.

'My head hurts,' Tom groaned weakly.

'I know. Don't worry, I'm going to fix it up.' Lee unfolded the scissors, hacked off a length of gauze and smeared it with cream. He laid it carefully over the cut. The blood soaked through immediately.

Lee picked up the bandage. His fingers were trembling so badly he couldn't remove the cellophane wrapper. He tore it open with his teeth and tossed it away. Then he began to wrap the bandage round Tom's forehead, covering the blood-soaked gauze.

The bandage slipped off. Lee swore under his breath. He tried again, lifting Tom up off the snow and propping him against his knee so he could wrap the bandage right round his head.

At first, blood from the cut soaked through the bandage. Lee wrapped it round again and again until the wound was completely covered. He pinned the end in place, hoping this would stop the blood oozing out. 'How do you feel now?' he asked shakily.

Tom's eyes opened. 'I'm not going any further, Lee,' he said, his voice cracking with despair. A fresh tear trickled down his cheek and he wiped it away. 'I can't walk any more. I'm too tired.'

'We'll stay here for a while until you feel better.' Lee tried to sound matter-of-fact about it, but a feeling of dread was throbbing through his head. They might have to spend the whole night out here, out on the mountain, with no shelter from the wind and snow. How could they survive in conditions like these?

Lee took Tom's hand. His own hands were chilled enough, but Tom's felt like a block of ice. Hurriedly Lee pushed it into his glove and fastened the wrist strap. Keeping warm was the most important thing now – he knew that.

Lee retrieved Tom's hat and goggles. He pocketed the goggles and cleared the snow out of the hat. Then he slid it over Tom's head, trying not to dislodge the bandage.

He laid Tom down again and stood up. 'I'm going to find us somewhere out of the wind,' he said. Tom didn't reply. Lee set off for the base of the cliff.

As he searched for the best place, he found his snowboard, half-buried in the snow. He pulled it out. Maybe, later, when Tom was settled out of the wind, he'd use it to head down to the road to fetch help. He glanced round quickly to see if he could locate Tom's board, but there was no sign of it.

The wind was blowing just as strongly beside the cliff as anywhere else on the slope, but Lee decided it might offer some protection from the driving snow. He laid his snowboard flat, close to the rocks, packing snow underneath to level it. Tom could sit on it while Lee worked out what to do. At least that way he'd be raised off the frozen snow.

He went back to Tom. He was sitting up, with his knees drawn up to his chest. His arms were wrapped round his legs and his eyes were closed. He was deathly pale and was shivering uncontrollably.

'You've got to stand up, Tom,' Lee said. Slipping his hands under his friend's armpits, he hauled him up and supported him as they made their way slowly up the slope. 'Sit here, on my snowboard.' He lowered Tom on to the makeshift seat. 'It'll keep you a bit dryer.'

The exercise seemed to revive Tom a little. 'I'm frozen, Lee,' he said, through chattering teeth. 'Maybe we *should* carry on to the road, after all.'

Lee shook his head. He was relieved that his friend was starting to sound more like himself, but he could still barely stand on his own. There was no way he'd be able to trek down the mountainside. 'Not yet.' He watched anxiously as Tom leant back against the rock and shut his eyes. 'I'm going to put your feet inside my backpack. That might warm them up a bit.'

Lee had read about snow survival techniques on the Internet, never dreaming he might actually need to put them into action. He tried to recall what he'd read about surviving in the open. Suddenly he remembered. He had to dig a snow-hole! People who were lost in the snow had survived by digging burrows to shelter in from bad weather.

Hurriedly Lee grabbed his backpack and lifted Tom's feet. He pushed them inside it and pulled up the drawstring to keep the snow out. Now he needed something that would keep Tom awake. It would be dangerous for his friend to fall asleep while he was so cold. Lee took his whistle out of the pocket of his backpack and held it in his hand for a moment. If Tom had to keep blowing it, he wouldn't be able to fall asleep. But the noise might trigger an avalanche. Lee tried to weigh up the risks.

In the end, he decided that the danger of Tom falling asleep and dying of cold was more immediate. He pushed the whistle into his friend's hand. 'Keep blowing this,' he said. 'That way, if anyone's about they'll hear it and know we're in trouble.'

Next, Lee took off his coat and draped it over his friend.

'What are you doing?' Tom cried, pushing it away. '*You* need this.'

'I'm going to be digging. We need a snow-hole. My fleece'll be plenty warm enough.' Lee tucked the coat round Tom again, then knelt down and began to burrow into the snow. The icy wind cut through his fleece, making him shiver, but he knew Tom needed the coat more than he did.

Darkness stole across the mountain while Lee was digging. Their surroundings lost their colour and took on a greyness that reflected his mood. Then, as the night swallowed everything up, he could see less and less, until eventually he could make out nothing at all.

He carried on digging, scooping out handfuls of snow and creating a deep hollow where they could shelter from the bitter wind. He talked to Tom as he worked. 'Marc will tell someone we're missing and they'll call out a mountain rescue team. They're probably on their way now. Make sure you keep a look out for them. And keep blowing that whistle.'

'Right.' The whistle shrilled. Lee paused for a moment to listen, terrified that he might hear the thundering roar of an avalanche. But nothing was to be heard except the buffeting of the wind in his ears.

'Jeff's probably cooking one of his stews to warm us up,' Lee said, 'so it might be better if we stay lost.' He laughed, trying to keep their spirits up.

Tom didn't join in.

'Don't go to sleep, Tom,' Lee warned.

'No,' his friend replied, but he sounded drowsy.

'Keep looking out for a light. And keep blowing that whistle.' Lee dug harder than ever: the snow-hole could be his friend's only chance of survival.

At last the snow-hole was finished. Lee sat back on his heels, wincing at the pain in his cramped and frozen legs. It was too dark now to see his watch, but he felt as though he'd been digging for hours. He stood up slowly and stretched, noticing for the first time that the wind had dropped and that an eerie silence had descended on the mountain. The snow still fell but, without the wind to drive it, it seemed a little less threatening.

'All done, Tom,' Lee said, flexing his aching arms. He couldn't see his friend in the darkness but he knew where he was from the regular shrilling of the whistle. Lee made his way across to him. 'How's your head now?'

'Throbbing.' Tom's teeth were chattering, even though he was still sheltering under Lee's coat.

Lee shook the snow off it, then helped him stand up. 'This snow-hole will help us keep warm.' As they made their way across to it, Lee noticed that Tom was shivering violently. Perhaps Tom was getting hypothermia, he thought fearfully. He knew people could die if their body temperature fell too low, but he didn't know how to warm his friend.

Lee helped Tom climb through the narrow opening of the snow cave, slide under the low snow roof and curl up on his side. When Tom was settled as comfortably as possible, Lee fetched his snowboard.

By now he was frozen to the core and he knew he'd have to put his coat on again. A pang of guilt swept over him: Tom needed his coat, too. In the end, Lee put it on but didn't fasten it. He slid down into his snowy burrow – there was just enough room for the two of them. He wedged the snowboard across the opening to keep out the drifting snow.

Lee turned awkwardly in the dark, confined space, then huddled against Tom's back, wrapping the front of his coat around his friend, hoping to warm him with the heat from his own body. 'I'm really sorry about all this, Tom,' he said.

'It's not your fault. The weather turning bad was just rotten luck.'

'It *is* my fault. I should never have suggested walking to the snowboard park. If we'd gone down to the village with Marc, we'd be safe and warm now.' He thought longingly of his bed at the chalet.

'I'm starving,' Tom said.

'Me too.' It was hours since they'd last eaten. 'Here,' Lee said. 'Finish off the water. There's not much left.'

Tom gratefully gulped down the last few mouthfuls of water. 'Do you think we'll be rescued?' Tom's voice quavered.

'Yes.' Lee spoke fiercely, as though he was trying to convince himself as well as his friend. 'A rescue team will be here first thing tomorrow, you'll see.'

But perhaps tomorrow would be too late. First they had to survive the long, cold night ahead of them.

CHAPTER EIGHT

That night seemed endless — the longest
Lee had ever known. And the coldest.
He lay awake in the snow-hole, clinging to
the hope that they'd live to see the morning.
Tom was sleeping beside him. He'd fallen
asleep almost as soon as they'd stopped talking
and Lee had been frightened when his friend
had first started to snore. He was pretty sure
that sleeping in the snow could lead to death.
But he knew, too, that Tom needed to rest.
Falling and cutting his head had shaken him
badly. If they were going to set off down the
mountain at first light, then he'd got to get
some sleep.

In the end, Lee had decided to watch over Tom. As long as he was snoring or breathing deeply, then he was probably OK. Lee would wake him only if his breathing became shallow or irregular.

He lay snuggled up against his friend and listened – listened to Tom's breathing and listened for the sounds of a rescue team: voices, whistles, the clatter of a helicopter's blades. He forced himself to keep his eyes open, staring blindly into the blackness so that he'd see the sudden brightness of the rescuers' torches. And he thought about their predicament. If only he hadn't been so keen to go to the snowboard park … If only they'd stayed in Chambeau or walked to the village with Marc to catch a cable car … It was his fault they were out here. And it would be his fault if they died. Tears welled up in his eyes.

If only the rescuers would come … if only … but nobody came. There was no sound from outside until the wind rose again and began to wail. And Lee was cold – so cold that his bones ached and every icy breath brought a sharp pain in his chest. Eventually, as the long night wore on, exhaustion overwhelmed him and he slept.

It was still dark when Lee woke up, but he knew at once where he was. He reached out for his friend, praying that he was OK. Tom moaned in his sleep, then began to snore. Relief coursed through Lee. Tom was still alive!

At last daylight came, grey and dismal, creeping into the snow cave. It came so gradually that, at first, Lee wasn't aware of it. It was only when he realized he could see the hump of Tom's shoulders that he knew the long night was finally over. He sat up stiffly, massaging his frozen, aching neck and shoulders, then pushed aside the snowboard that blocked the entrance and peered out. It was still snowing.

He turned back to his friend. No matter what the weather, they were going to get off the mountain today. He shook Tom's shoulder, calling his name.

Tom woke suddenly. 'What's wrong?' he demanded.

'Nothing. It's morning. How's your head?'

Tom fingered his bandage and winced. 'A bit sore.'

'We ought to get going. Are you up to it?'

Tom sat up, rubbing his arms. 'I'll be OK once we're moving.'

'There's probably a nice, warm café five minutes' walk from here,' Lee said, crawling outside. *I wish*, he thought, his mouth watering as he pictured the two of them tucking into bacon sandwiches and hot chocolate.

Tom followed him, bringing the backpack. 'I hope you're right.'

Lee stood up shakily. He felt weak with hunger and cold, but he slung the rucksack on his back and tucked his snowboard under his arm. Tom looked around. 'Where's my board?'

'I don't know. I couldn't find it last night.' Lee shook his head. 'I'm sorry, Tom.'

Tom shrugged. 'I probably won't want to snowboard again after this, anyway.'

'You can share mine,' Lee said, 'and –' He broke off suddenly and pointed to a bush a little way down the slope. 'It's there, look, stuck in that bush.'

They tramped down the slope and retrieved the snowboard, checking that it wasn't damaged. Then they set off on foot down the mountainside, moving cautiously through the whirling snow, both well aware of the dangers that falling would bring.

Their progress was painfully slow. They hadn't eaten since they'd shared Lee's chocolate the day before, and now they were close to exhaustion. The new snow was soft and deep; in places, they sank waist-deep into it and had to use vital energy helping each other out. Even on firmer snow, each plodding, shaky step was a massive effort.

'If only it'd stop snowing,' Lee groaned after they'd been trudging along for nearly an hour. 'At least we'd be able to see where we were going.' The journey was turning into a repeat of yesterday's nightmare, with the wind buffeting them and the snow lashing across their faces.

'Surely we've got to reach the road soon,' Tom said weakly. 'I don't know how much longer I can go on.'

Lee knew what he meant. He was dangerously close to giving up, too. Pushing himself on and on through the snow, knowing they were getting nowhere, was almost too great an effort now. His legs hurt, his chest hurt, his body ached with hunger and he was cold. So cold. He just wanted to lie down and sleep.

He cleared his goggles and peered into the swirling snowstorm, hoping to spot something that would give him the impetus to carry on.

'I've had it,' Tom said, sinking into the snow.

'No!' Lee knelt beside his friend. 'We've got to keep going, Tom.'

Tom shook his head wearily. 'What's the point? We're never going to get anywhere.'

Lee stared past him. Perhaps Tom was right. Perhaps he was fooling himself if he thought they stood a chance of survival.

Suddenly his heartbeat quickened. There was somebody out there. He'd seen a dark figure moving, he was sure of it. The wind gusted fiercely, blocking his view with a flurry of wildly dancing snowflakes.

Lee continued to stare at the place where the figure had been, hope burning fiercely inside him. 'Tom! There's someone there!' He raised his voice, heedless of the danger of starting an avalanche. 'Help! Help! We're lost! Help!' The wind snatched his words away. He listened intently, hoping to hear an answering shout. There wasn't one. He shouted again.

Tom struggled to his feet and joined in, but there was still no reply.

'It's too windy,' Lee cried desperately. 'They can't hear us.' He floundered up the slope towards the place where he'd seen the movement. Tom followed.

As they climbed, Lee saw the figure again. It was moving away from them and at a speed much quicker than they could manage. 'Wait!' Lee screamed, suddenly terrified that this lifeline was about to be snatched away from them.

The figure kept going. Lee remembered the whistle. 'The whistle, Tom!' he cried. 'Blow the whistle!' He watched in agitation as Tom plunged his hand into his pocket and pulled it out. He raised it to his lips and blew. The shrill note cut through the howl of the wind. The distant figure hesitated, then turned slowly as though trying to see through the snowstorm.

Tom blew the whistle again. Lee stumbled uphill with Tom close on his heels. The figure hurried towards them. They could see now that he or she was carrying a pair of skis on his or her shoulder.

'Jeff!' Lee cried, as the figure emerged through the blinding snow.

'And Dominique!' Tom shouted, as a second figure appeared.

'Thank God!' Jeff dropped his skis, ran to the boys and flung his arms round them. 'Are you both all right?'

'Very tired and cold,' Tom replied.

'We were so worried about you.' Jeff's voice was hoarse with emotion. He tilted Lee's head back and scanned his face. 'I can hardly believe we've found you. I thought …' His eyes glittered with tears. 'Being out all night like that …'

'We sheltered in a snow-hole,' Lee said.

'Did you?' Jeff's face lit up with admiration. 'Did you hear that, Dominique? They dug a snow-hole to keep themselves alive. That's brilliant!'

Dominique was rummaging in her backpack. 'Tom's head is cut,' she said.

Jeff turned to see. 'What happened?' he asked anxiously, eyeing Tom's blood-stained bandage.

'I fell over a cliff.'

The colour drained out of Jeff's face. 'You did *what*?'

Dominique pulled out a first-aid kit. 'I'll look at his cut, Jeff. You pour them some hot milk and give them chocolate.'

They crouched behind a nearby bush, out of the wind. Dominique had re-bandaged Tom's head and now the boys were sipping their hot milk gratefully, relishing its warmth.

'How did you find us?' Lee asked, swallowing a mouthful of chocolate. He was feeling better already and could hardly believe that he'd been close to giving up just a short while before.

'Your friend Marc contacted the Mountain Rescue Centre when the storm started,' Jeff explained. 'They got in touch with us to see if you'd made it home.'

'Are they out looking for us, then?' Tom asked. 'We haven't seen anyone else.'

'There was no rescue team available,' Dominique said. She pulled a radio out of her backpack. 'Should we let them know we've found the boys and that we're all OK?' she asked. 'Or would it be better to wait until we've got them off the mountain?'

'Wait a while,' Jeff said. 'We're not exactly safe yet.'

'Why wasn't there a rescue team?' Lee asked. 'I thought they were always willing to come out.'

'They're out already,' Jeff said. 'This weather's caused a whole spate of avalanches. Everyone's been working virtually non-stop to get people out. Marc said you were heading for the snowboard park, so we guessed you'd be somewhere on a line between the park and the bus.'

'Hasn't the bus been towed away, then?' Lee asked.

Jeff shook his head. 'There's been an avalanche near Val Thorens. Nobody's hurt, but the road's totally blocked so the breakdown truck can't get through.'

Dominique squeezed Jeff's arm. 'Jeff sat up all night, hoping you'd come back. We left very early this morning so we could start searching for you as soon as it got light.'

'Thanks.' Lee flashed Jeff a grateful smile. Even though they argued most of the time, he knew he could always rely on his brother when it came to the crunch.

'Yeah, thanks,' said Tom as he finished his second cup of milk.

'Put these on,' Dominique said. She pulled

dry jumpers, gloves and hats out of her backpack. 'Then we'll go home.'

'It's not very far to the road from here,' Jeff said. He took out a compass and checked the direction.

Wearily, the boys changed into dry clothes. Dominique put the wet ones into her backpack.

'Let's go, then,' Jeff said. The snow had almost stopped and a pale sun was struggling to break through the leaden clouds.

'We might be able to board down, now we can see where we're going,' Lee said. The quicker they got off the mountain, the better he'd like it. Even though the hot milk and chocolate had revived him a little, he was still utterly exhausted. All he wanted to do was crawl into a warm bed and rest his aching body.

'We need to be careful,' Jeff warned. 'There's so much loose snow about that there's a big risk of starting an avalanche.' He looked up at the sky, and an expression of concern crossed his face. 'We don't want to hang about, though. There's a lot more snow to come by the look of those clouds.'

CHAPTER NINE

They started down the mountain. Jeff went first, on his skis, with Tom close behind him. Lee came next, and Dominique brought up the rear. The boys carried their snowboards.

Lee thought about the lucky escape they'd had. If Jeff and Dominique hadn't shown up when they did ... if he hadn't spotted them through the snow ... if he hadn't brought a whistle ... He gave himself a mental shake. There was no point dwelling on what might have happened when everything was going to be OK now.

They came out from behind a cluster of

trees – and there at last was the road below them, with the crashed bus still slewed across it. Behind it was Jeff's car. Away in the distance, along the road to Chambeau, a snow-plough was chugging, throwing out a cloud of black exhaust fumes.

A wave of relief swept over Lee. They were almost out of this mess! After all they'd been through, they'd finally made it. He smiled shakily at Tom.

Lee watched his brother survey the landscape, trying to figure out the easiest route to take. Directly below them was a smooth slope of freshly laid, untouched snow. 'We don't want to go that way,' Jeff said. 'It's too steep. That's a classic avalanche risk slope.'

'But it looks the quickest way down,' Lee said. Beyond the slope was a field dotted with rocks and, below that, was the road.

'No, it's too dangerous,' Jeff said. 'We'll cross the top of this slope, keeping close to that wall of rock. Then we'll see if we can find a safer way down.'

'Is it much further?' Tom asked. 'My head's killing me.'

'We'll soon be down,' Dominique promised him.

They went on across the mountain to their right, keeping close to the foot of a cliff. The sky grew darker and the wind picked up. Lee shivered. He was certain it was going to snow again. Even Jeff and Dominique might not be able to find a way off the mountain in a snowstorm. His spirits plummeted. He was too exhausted to spend another day clambering up and down, trying to find a way to the road. And suppose they had to spend a second night out of doors?

Soon the ground became rocky. Jeff and Dominique took off their skis, and they all clambered over the slippery rocks, slipping and sliding awkwardly as they headed downhill. Eventually they reached a broad sweep of unbroken snow.

Jeff drew in his breath sharply. 'It's too steep, like that other one. We could set off an avalanche if we try to cross this one too.'

'But what else can we do?' Lee groaned, slumping down on a rock. The thought of having to go back was more than he could bear. He looked up the mountain. The slope seemed to go on almost for ever in that direction, and it ended, a long way above them, in a clump of dark pine trees. He couldn't possibly raise the energy to climb all the way up there.

He looked downhill. The slope ended in a sheer drop, so they couldn't go straight down. But further on – if they could cross the steep bit – the slope became more gentle. Lee surveyed it hopefully. It appeared to run almost to the road.

Dominique sighed. 'We'll have to risk crossing this steep place, Jeff. The boys are worn out. We must get them home.' Snow began to fall again. 'And besides, this area has so many steep slopes. Even if we find a way round this one, we'll have to cross another somewhere else.'

Jeff nodded in resignation. 'We'll cross one at a time,' he said. 'Dominique and I will ski. You two'll have to use your snowboards. Will you be able to manage that? We need to get across here as quickly as we can.'

'We'll be OK, won't we, Tom?' Lee said, glancing at his friend.

Tom smiled uncertainly. 'I suppose so.'

'Good. We'll cross diagonally because it's less risky,' Jeff said.

He and Dominique started to discuss the angle of the slope and the safest direction to take.

'If you find yourself caught up in an avalanche,' Jeff said, turning back to the boys, 'try and swim in the snow so that you stay on top of it. And steer yourself round rocks and stuff.'

Dominique jumped up and down on the edge of the slope. 'This bit seems stable,' she said.

'Good.' Jeff turned to the boys again. 'Try and keep your head up the slope and your feet lower if you *do* get swept away. When you feel yourself slowing down, stick your arm up so we can find you.'

'And cup your other hand in front of your mouth so you have an air space,' Dominique added.

Lee's stomach began to churn with fear. Jeff and Dominique appeared to be seriously worried – they made it sound as though an avalanche was unavoidable. 'What are our chances of getting across safely?' he asked.

Jeff shrugged. 'I don't know, but it's best to know the safety drill, even if we don't have to use it.'

Lee looked up the slope, imagining how it would feel to see all that snow plunging towards him. He'd heard that an avalanche could travel at well over a hundred kilometres an hour.

'Right,' Jeff said briskly. 'Dominique's going first. You'll go next, Tom. Then you, Lee, and I'll come last.'

'Don't put the leash of your snowboards on,' Dominique advised them. 'If you do get caught in a slide, try to ditch your board so it doesn't drag you down.'

'Right, then.' Jeff turned to Dominique. 'Good luck.'

Lee's heart began to pound as he watched Dominique ski expertly across the slope. He willed her to make it to the other side, making a mental note of the line she took: he'd have to follow it himself in a few minutes. When she was halfway across, the snow, which was falling harder now, blocked his view of her.

'Oh, this is hopeless!' Jeff groaned. He rounded on Lee. 'I warned you not to go to that wretched snowboard park. But would you listen to me?'

Lee bit back an angry retort. He knew Jeff was worried. And he'd been pretty good about the whole incident up till now. 'Sorry,' he said. 'The weather looked fine when we set off.'

'Yes, well ...' Jeff looked at Tom. 'Your turn now.'

Tom fastened on his snowboard and stood up. His face was almost as white as the snow and his eyes were dark with anxiety. 'I've got to follow Dominique's tracks, right?'

'That's right.'

'Just traverse across,' Lee said encouragingly. 'It'll be an easy run.'

Tom gulped. 'What if I fall over, though? I'm bound to start an avalanche if I do. And I'll go over that cliff at the bottom.'

'You won't fall.' Lee gave him a gentle shove. 'Go on, get out there and stop worrying.'

Tom squared his shoulders and set off across the slope. In a few seconds, he had disappeared in the swirling snow.

Jeff turned to Lee. 'Remember to stick to a diagonal line,' he said. 'No showing off. No ...'

'I'm not a total idiot, Jeff.'

'I know that. But I can't help worrying about you.' He rested a hand on Lee's shoulder. 'Be careful.'

Lee nodded. 'You too.' He jumped his board round then rode out across the slope, crouching low so he could see the tracks

Dominique and Tom had left. He rode quickly, trying not to think about avalanches. He knew the theory of what to do if he was caught in one, but he wasn't sure that he could actually put it into practice when the time came. What if he forgot everything in his panic at being swept away?

Stop it, he told himself sharply. *There's not going to be an avalanche. You're going to cross this slope safely*. He wiped away the snow that was collecting on his goggles and rode on.

Suddenly he felt himself slipping sideways downhill. He leant back hard on the heel edge of his board, trying to slow himself. It didn't do any good. If anything, he was moving more quickly. But that didn't make sense. He looked down at his board and his heart missed a beat. No wonder he couldn't slow down. The snow was sliding with him. He'd started a mini-avalanche. Panic coursed through him. He was riding an avalanche and he couldn't stop!

Lee's heart pounded frantically. He couldn't think, he could barely even breathe. He was careering along. Snow sprayed up and the wind was cutting through his clothes. And his head was hammering with fear.

He thought about Jeff. He'd be waiting to cross the slope. Lee had to warn him. 'I'm in an avalanche, Jeff!' he shrieked. 'Don't cross the slope! Don't cross ...' Snow flew up into his mouth, silencing him. He spat it out and prayed that Jeff had heard him.

The avalanche swept him on so fast that it blurred his surroundings. He could see nothing but rushing whiteness in every direction. He fought down his fear and tried to remember some details of the terrain, hoping that the knowledge would help him survive. There were rocks to his left and a broad gentle slope to his right that led down to the road. And below this slope ... An icy hand clutched his heart. Below this slope, there was a cliff edge. If he didn't manage to stop, he'd be carried over it.

Lee's mind was in turmoil as he rocketed along. How far would he fall? He'd probably survive a drop of three or four metres. But any more than that ...

The snowboard wobbled. Lee flung his arms out, fighting desperately to stay upright. A moment later he toppled over and sank into the rushing snow. *Swim to the surface.* Survival instructions echoed inside his head. He battled to get out of the churning, frothing snow, working his arms furiously. But his snowboard was dragging him down.

He hunched over, reaching for his bindings. He released his front foot easily enough. But now his board seemed to be developing a mind of its own. It twisted away, hauling Lee around by his right foot and rolling him over and over. He couldn't see anything. He could barely breathe. Snow was in his mouth and nose. It was in his ears.

He twisted around, reaching for his snowboard, fighting down his terror. If he could just release his back foot ... if he could get himself to the surface ... His fingers brushed the board. He seized it. Feeling his way along it, still rolling, he found his foot. The binding was clogged up with snow. Lee wrenched at the strap. And suddenly his foot was free.

A split second later, he felt himself plummeting downwards. He'd gone over the edge! Almost at once, he landed heavily on his back and snow crashed down on top of him. Instinctively, he stuck up an arm and cupped his other hand in front of his mouth.

He was buried in the snow.

Lee could feel it lying on him like a cold, thick, heavy blanket. He opened his eyes, hoping he'd see a glimmer of daylight, but his goggles were totally covered in snow.

Struggling to keep calm, he scraped out a small cavity above his goggles, then cleared the snow from them. The effort was wasted because all he could see was whiteness. Fear grew inside him. Battling it down, he tried desperately to move. The weight of the snow held him rigid. His legs were pressed hard together, cocooned in snow that had set like concrete. The hand in front of his face had a little space to move but his other arm, which was extended above him, was completely trapped.

Terror filled him. He had to get out! He flexed his muscles and arched his back, straining to get free ... it was hopeless. Nothing did any good. He'd never escape. Fighting back tears, he shut his eyes and forced himself to take slow, calming breaths. He had limited air, and panicking would use it up quickly. But lying in this cold, silent darkness was worse than any nightmare. He was buried alive! And if his air ran out before the others found him, he'd die there. Alone.

CHAPTER TEN

It seemed an age before Lee heard footsteps above him. 'I'm here!' he screamed. 'Help! Help!' But he wasn't sure they'd be able to hear him. The wind would be blowing hard on the surface and they might well be talking to each other, too, drowning out his muffled shouts.

The footsteps moved away. Lee yelled again, willing them to return.

'What's this?' It was Tom's voice, sounding distant and distorted.

'I'm here!' Lee cried.

'He must be here,' Tom said. 'He wouldn't go far from his snowboard, if he could help it.'

Lee heard Dominique's voice reply, but he

couldn't work out what she'd said. He waited tensely. At last he heard scraping coming from somewhere to his right. They were digging in the snow, trying to find him. His spirits lifted. Jeff and Dominique must have brought a spade with them. They were going to get him out.

Lee waited impatiently until there was a break in the digging, knowing they wouldn't hear him above the sound of the spade cutting through the snow. Then he called again: 'I'm here! Down here!'

'What was that?' Dominique's voice was clearer now.

'What?' Tom asked.

'I thought I heard something.'

Lee shouted again: 'Tom! Dominique!'

'Lee! Call again so we can find you,' Tom cried excitedly.

'Here! I'm here!'

'Got you!' The scraping started again, above his head this time.

As he lay waiting for rescue, Lee realized that he hadn't heard Jeff's voice. Dismay gripped him. What if Jeff had also been caught in the avalanche? 'Where's Jeff?' he yelled.

The digging above his head continued.

'Where's Jeff?' he cried again.

There was still no reply. They obviously couldn't hear him. He'd have to wait until they broke through to find out if his brother was OK.

The waiting was terrible. The noise of the spade grew louder. A cold, bluish light filtered into Lee's snowy prison. Gradually the light increased. Tiny droplets of snow drifted down on to his face. His impatience grew. He had to find out about Jeff.

The spade was almost through above his head. He could see its dark shadow now, appearing and disappearing through the snow. He called out: 'You're getting close. Watch out.'

The spade drew back and a hand replaced it, scraping the snow away. At last they broke through, letting grey light and suffocating snow flood in. Coughing, Lee brushed it away from his face. He helped to enlarge the hole until he could see Tom's anxious face above him. He was holding a small shovel. 'Are you OK?' his friend asked. 'Any bones broken?'

'Where's Jeff?' Lee's teeth were chattering furiously – though whether from cold or fear he couldn't tell.

'Over there.' Tom turned away for a moment. 'He heard you shout and he set off after you, but he got caught up in a second avalanche. It looks like he's broken his ankle.'

'But he's OK?'

'Yeah. I suppose so.'

As he clambered out of the snow, Lee breathed a sigh of relief. He and Jeff had been caught up in an avalanche but they'd both survived.

Jeff was sitting at the base of the cliff. Dominique was bending over him, doing something to his ankle.

Lee unfastened his coat and shook the snow out of his clothes. They were soaking wet, but he'd have to put up with it. Shivering, he did his coat up again and went across to Jeff. 'How do you feel?' he asked.

His brother smiled weakly. 'I've been better. How about you?'

Lee nodded. 'I'm all right. Just cold and wet.' He turned away so they wouldn't see the tears that had filled his eyes. He'd really believed he was going to die under the snow and, now he was safe, the shock of the experience seemed to have caught up with him. His hands trembled violently and he clasped them tightly together, trying to still them.

'I've radioed Mountain Rescue, but there's been another big avalanche,' Dominique said. 'Nobody's available to get us off the mountain.'

'It's not far, though,' Tom pointed out. 'Look how close we are to the bus.' They were at the top of a fairly gentle slope that led down to the road. The bus was directly below them and, behind it, Lee could see Jeff's car. The sight of it cheered him. With any luck, they'd be on their way home soon. He blinked away his tears and pulled his coat more tightly round himself, trying to get some warmth into his frozen body. His teeth chattered uncontrollably.

'How am I going to get down there?' Jeff said. 'I can hardly walk or ski like this.' Dominique had tied bandages round both his legs, at ankle and knee, so his good leg would act as a splint for the broken one.

'We could carry you,' Tom suggested doubtfully.

'Or you could sit on one of our snowboards and slide down,' Lee suggested, relieved to turn his thoughts to a practical problem. 'If we tied something to the back binding, we could hold on to it so that it wouldn't go too fast.'

Jeff frowned. 'I'm not sure.'

'What else can we do?' Dominique said. 'We can't leave you here.'

'And if there's no rescue team coming, we've got to get you down ourselves,' Lee said. He fetched his snowboard, which was lying on top of the drift he'd been dug out of. 'Can you get yourself on to it, Jeff? Or shall we lift you?'

Dominique pulled Lee's wet fleece out of her rucksack and tied it to the back binding as Jeff hauled himself on to the snowboard.

They started down the slope towards the bus, with Dominique and Lee holding the sleeves of the fleece to prevent the snowboard from running away with Jeff. Tom carried both pairs of skis and his own snowboard. Lee watched the bus as they walked. They were getting nearer and nearer to it, and with every step his hopes rose. They were getting off the mountain at last.

They were only a few metres from the bus when Lee heard a strange noise behind him – a hissing, roaring noise. He twisted round to see what it was and his blood ran cold. A great, frothing wall of whiteness was tearing down the mountainside towards them. 'Avalanche!' he yelled.

The others turned fearfully, their eyes widening with horror. 'It's a big one! Get in the car! Quick!' Jeff cried.

'There's no time!' Dominique screamed. The avalanche was hurtling down the mountainside, moving as fast as an express train.

'The bus!' Lee yelled. 'It's our only chance.' He, Tom and Dominique heaved Jeff upright. With him between them, they ran to the bus, gasping with effort and with terror. The door stood open. They humped him inside and laid him down on the floor between the seats.

The avalanche was almost upon them – all Lee could see through the windows was a tidal wave of foaming snow. 'Get down!' he shrieked. 'And hold on to the legs of the seats.' He hunched down, clinging tightly to the iron supports, his head tucked under a seat for protection.

The wall of snow hit the bus with a force that shoved it across the road and made them cry out. It smashed the remaining windows and poured inside, burying the four frightened occupants. Blinded by snow, Lee felt the bus rock dangerously. He tightened his grip on the seat supports, terrified that it would plunge down the mountainside.

The bus tilted, swinging him around and clear of the snow for a moment. To his horror, he saw that the bus was almost on its side, teetering in mid-air while more and more snow poured in through the windows. Then, with a great grinding and creaking of metal, it rolled over.

CHAPTER ELEVEN

The snow enveloped Lee, forcing its way under his collar and up his sleeves. The bus rolled again, on to its roof this time, with a violent jolt. A moment later it began moving in earnest, gathering speed. The avalanche had swept it off the road, and now it was skidding down the mountainside.

Lee's heart was thumping so hard he thought it would burst through his chest. His breath was coming in jerky gasps. He clung to the chair supports, but he knew he wouldn't be able to hold on for much longer. As the bus shook, his arms were being wrenched almost out of their sockets and his chest was being pounded painfully against the side of the seat.

At last the bus slowed and came to a rest; an eerie silence descended.

Lee opened his eyes.

The bus was upside down. The seats were hanging down above him and the roof below him was covered in deep snow, sprinkled with shards of glass from the smashed windows. His legs were pulled up, clear of the snow, though he couldn't remember lifting them. His hands, immobilized by fear, were locked round one of the seat supports.

It was gloomy in the bus. So much snow had come inside that the windows were covered; but, as Lee's eyes adjusted to the poor light, he realized that there was no sign of the others. 'Where are you?' he screamed. 'Jeff! Dominique! Tom! Where are you?'

There was no reply – but he knew the answer anyway. They were somewhere below him, buried in the snow.

Lee let his feet drop down. He sank ankle-deep into the snow. Then he let go of the seat support: he had to dig them out. And quickly.

As he lowered his arms, a knife-like pain stabbed through his chest, making him gasp.

He groaned: he recognized the pain. He'd felt one just like it when he'd cracked two ribs playing football a couple of years ago.

For a few moments the pain was so agonizing that he couldn't move. When it subsided a little, he looked around wildly, trying desperately to locate the others. Halfway down the bus he saw a splash of brilliant red. For a horrifying, heart-lurching moment he thought it was blood, then he realized it was the strap of Jeff's rucksack.

Lee looked beyond it. A boot was sticking out of the snow. With a shock of recognition he realized it was Tom's. There was no sign of Jeff or Dominique.

Lee crawled shakily towards Tom's foot, gritting his teeth against the pain in his chest. Glass stabbed his knees. Wincing, he forced himself to his feet and brushed the glass away with his gloved hands. Spots of blood soaked through his trouser legs, but there was no time to worry about minor cuts now. He stumbled to Tom's foot and touched it. Relief surged inside him as he felt it move. Tom was alive!

'I'll get you out, Tom!' Lee cried. He scrabbled at the snow, his padded gloves protecting his hands from the glass. At first the snow came away in a flurry of white powder but, as he dug further, it became more solid. By the time he'd uncovered Tom's leg to the knee, it was as hard as rock; his fingers could make no impression on it. He needed the shovel Jeff and Dominique had brought with them.

He limped across to Jeff's rucksack and hauled it out of the snow. With trembling fingers he unfastened it. The shovel was there. He pulled it out. He was going to get them out.

He staggered back to Tom and began to dig again, heedless of the pain in his chest. He had to work quickly. Tom could be short of air, and he still had to find the others.

It seemed an age before Lee uncovered his friend. He peered into the hole he had made, willing him to be all right. 'Tom!' he cried.

Tom's eyes flickered open. His face was grey, his bandage had come off and the cut on his head was bleeding again, but he managed to smile. He struggled to his feet. 'Dominique's down here, too,' he said. 'She's underneath me. She spoke to me when the bus first stopped rolling, but since then she hasn't said anything for ages.'

Wincing at the pain in his chest, Lee helped Tom climb out of the hole.

'What's up?' Tom asked. 'Are you hurt?'

'I think I've cracked a rib. I just need to keep still for a minute. I'll feel better soon.' Lee crouched down, waiting helplessly for the pain to subside, angry at wasting valuable time. He could see Dominique's back below, her yellow jacket gleaming in the dim light. She wasn't moving.

'Dominique, can you hear me?' Tom called.

There was no reply.

'We've got to get her out,' Lee said, as his pain eased a little. He climbed down into the hole, planting his feet on either side of Dominique. He slid his arms round her and tried to lift her, doubling over as another wave of pain swept though him. The weight of the snow held her tightly in place. 'Dominique!' he cried. She didn't stir.

'Throw me the shovel, Tom,' Lee said urgently. He dug feverishly, working towards her head, knowing they'd got to get her out quickly. If it wasn't already too late …

The two boys worked frantically, driven by desperation, their weariness forgotten. They were in a race against time. Lee dug down from the surface with the shovel, slicing through the frozen snow and heaving it aside, though every movement sent a fresh wave of pain through him. Sweat dripped down his forehead, but he didn't dare stop to take off his coat. There wasn't time for that. They'd got to free Dominique and then search for Jeff.

Tom knelt in the hole, straddling Dominique's back. Using the screwdriver from Lee's tool kit, he was chipping away at the snow which lay directly on top of her. He hacked out a biggish chunk of snow and threw it out of the hole.

They uncovered her at last. She was lying awkwardly, with her face turned to one side. Her wet hair clung to her head. Lee bent over her. 'Dominique,' he said urgently.

She didn't stir.

'Is she all right?' Tom asked quaveringly.

Lee took off his gloves. He reached out a shaking hand and touched her cheek. It was red raw and icy cold. Swallowing hard, he pushed his fingers inside her collar, feeling for a pulse. He found nothing.

CHAPTER TWELVE

Tears filled Lee's eyes. 'Dominique,' he sobbed.

'Oh God.' Tom's voice was little more than a whisper.

Lee bit his lip, trying to stop it trembling. Then he felt a tiny flutter beneath his fingers. He moved them slightly and felt it again, stronger this time. She *did* have a pulse. 'She's not dead!' he cried jubilantly.

'I'll lift her out.' Tom climbed into the hole.

'Wait,' Lee said. 'I don't know if we should lift her. Not while she's unconscious.'

'We can't leave her lying here in this hole,' Tom said. He held Dominique under the armpits, dragged her out on to the surface of the snow and laid her down. 'She's still unconscious but she's breathing OK.' He knelt beside her and patted her hand.

Clutching his chest, Lee climbed out of the hole. A faint flush of colour was stealing into Dominique's face. Lee took off his coat and laid it over her. Then he surveyed the bus anxiously, hoping to find some clue to his brother's whereabouts. They'd got to find Jeff quickly. There was no way of knowing where he was, though. Everything was covered in deep snow.

'Jeff,' he called. 'Where are you?' His voice echoed shrilly.

He held his breath, listening eagerly. The wind howled outside and the bus creaked. 'Jeff!' he called again.

The wind dropped for a moment, and in the sudden silence he thought he could hear a faint voice. 'Jeff!' Lee dropped to his knees and pressed his ear to the snow.

'Lee, get me out.' Jeff's voice was muffled.

Tom came running with the shovel. Lee seized it and plunged it into the snow. He dug furiously, his fear for his brother giving him the strength to ignore his pain. Tom set to work with the screwdriver again.

They found Jeff's arm first, sticking straight up through the snow. Lee touched his hand and was relieved to feel it grip him tightly. 'We'll have you out in a minute,' he called.

'Good. It's freezing down here.'

The boys dug more carefully now. They didn't want to injure Jeff with their tools. At last they uncovered a patch of blue: Jeff's coat. They scraped away more snow until they could see his face.

'Is Dominique OK?' he asked. He sat up, wincing.

'Are you hurt?' Lee asked anxiously, ignoring the question.

'Only my ankle. Is Dominique all right?'

Lee glanced at Dominique. She hadn't moved, but the coat he'd lain over her was rising and falling in time with her breathing.

'Well?' Jeff demanded, struggling to pull himself out of the snow.

'She's unconscious, but I think she'll be OK.'

They sat round Dominique in a shocked, silent huddle. Lee felt drained. Fear for his companions' safety had kept him going before, but now he couldn't stop thinking how badly his chest hurt.

'She must have hit her head,' Jeff said at last, feeling for a bump under Dominique's hair. 'We'll have to get a rescue team in quickly. She ought to be in hospital.'

Lee rummaged wearily in Jeff's rucksack for the radio. He pulled it out but the front of it was staved in. 'It's broken,' he said.

'Give it here.' Jeff pressed the switch. Nothing happened. He shook the radio hard but it was completely dead.

'Dominique made a call after the first avalanche,' Tom said. 'Mountain Rescue know we're out here.'

'They think we're up the mountain, on the other side of the road,' Jeff said in consternation. 'They probably won't spot us down here.' He pressed the buttons on the radio again, but it still wouldn't work. 'If only we'd brought a distress beacon. They'd have been able to pinpoint us then. But when I went to get one from the ski-lodge, all the beacons had gone. Most of the instructors have gone out with Mountain Rescue teams and they'd all taken one.' He frowned. 'We had to come, though, even without the proper equipment. We could hardly have left you two out here on your own.'

Lee felt a twinge of guilt. He'd caused so much trouble. He stood up. 'We'll have to make the Mountain Rescue people notice us.' He picked up Jeff's rucksack and hobbled towards the door, clutching his ribs.

'Where are you going?' Jeff asked.

'Outside. I'm going to watch out for the rescue team. And this bag's bright enough to be seen a mile off.'

'Take your coat,' Jeff said.

Lee hesitated. It was going to be freezing outside. He'd need his coat. But Dominique had to be kept warm, too. 'I'll be all right,' he said.

'Do as you're told,' Jeff insisted. 'Put your coat on.' He lifted it carefully off Dominique and flung it at Lee. 'And wear this as well.' Jeff tossed him his hat. Lee put them on. Then he headed for the door, ducking to get through because the snow, both inside and out, was piled so high.

The icy wind hit Lee as soon as he emerged from the bus. Shivering, he turned up his collar and looked around. It had stopped snowing and the sky was blue.

Lee shuffled painfully along the broad ridge of snow that had built up between the half-buried bus and a line of rocks that crossed the slope. Below him, the path of the avalanche was marked by snapped-off tree trunks. A long way down, in the bottom of the valley, was a mound of snow and other debris the size of a mini-mountain. He felt the colour drain from his face. If it hadn't been for those rocks, the bus would have gone right to the bottom, taking them with it.

The bus lay on its roof, covered in a thick blanket of snow. More snow had piled up along the far side of the bus. Lee could see whole trees and sizeable boulders mixed in with it. He climbed up on top of the bus, both to get a better view and to be seen more easily by any rescuers.

He looked up beyond the heaped-up snow and picked out the road. They were about a hundred metres below it. Jeff's car wasn't there: it must have been swept down the mountainside.

'Can you see anyone?'

Lee looked around. Tom was standing behind him. 'Not yet,' Lee said. 'How's your head?'

Tom shrugged. 'Bearable.' He clambered up beside Lee.

'Dominique's awake!' Jeff suddenly called from inside the bus.

'Is she OK?'

'Yeah. Apart from a bit of a headache.'

A great wave of relief washed over Lee. 'Thank God.' He'd been so frightened that she wouldn't make it. He looked up the mountain again, at the broad path of destruction the avalanche had left in its wake.

The two boys crouched down side by side, trying to get out of the wind. Tom pointed towards the village. 'Do you think we should try walking to Val des Pins? We might be able to get help there.'

Lee looked at the distant houses. They were so far away that they could have been miniature buildings from a small-gauge train set. And the journey would be impossibly difficult with so many hills of snow to clamber over – especially when moving was so painful.

He shook his head. The idea of reaching warmth, safety and food was overwhelmingly appealing, but he knew it would be a dangerous journey. They were too exhausted to travel so far, and his cracked ribs would make walking agony. And besides, they might start another avalanche. Lee shuddered. He'd already survived two. The third time he might not be so lucky. 'We're better off staying here,' he said.

Surely the Mountain Rescue team would come soon.

It was bitterly cold, but Lee and Tom stayed on top of the bus and watched the road, huddling together for warmth.

From time to time Jeff called up to them, telling them to come inside the bus and get warm, but they were determined to stay where they were. The thought of missing the rescue team was too awful.

Suddenly Lee spotted a movement on the road. 'What's that?'

A figure in an orange coat and black hat had rounded the corner on the road above. He was carrying a large pack. More people came into view.

'They're here!' Lee lurched painfully to his feet. He wanted to wave and attract their attention but the pain in his ribs was too intense. He doubled over.

Tom scrambled up, waving his arms wildly. The rescuers were looking up the mountainside, away from them, pointing towards the snowboard park.

'We're here!' Tom screeched.

The rescue team didn't hear him. They were still looking uphill.

Tom pulled off his glove and thrust his hand into his pocket. He found the whistle. Putting it to his lips, he blew hard. The man at the front of the rescue team stopped and looked back.

'They've heard it,' Lee cried. 'Blow it again.'

The whistle shrilled once more. The men turned slowly, searching for them.

Tom waved frantically, jumping up and down. Lee watched helplessly, praying that the men would spot them.

He saw somebody pointing, then the team came hurrying towards them, scrambling over the heaped-up snow.

Jeff's voice floated up from inside the bus. 'What's happening?'

'They've found us.' Lee was almost crying with relief.

They were safe. Their ordeal was almost over.

★

The hospital was quiet. Lee lay in his bed, deliciously warm, listening to the wind outside. A doctor had examined him and announced that two of his ribs were cracked, but Lee knew that was a minor price to pay for getting caught in an avalanche.

In the bed next to him, Tom was already asleep, the cut on his forehead already stitched and dressed. Lee could hear his deep breathing.

Jeff and Dominique were in adult wards, somewhere upstairs. Jeff's ankle had been plastered, and the nurses were keeping an eye on Dominique because she'd been knocked out. But it was the fact that they were so cold that had prompted the doctor to keep them all in hospital.

Lee was unbelievably tired but, now he was finally in bed, sleep wouldn't come. His head was whirling with the events of the last two days. He knew they'd had an incredibly lucky escape.

A nurse tiptoed down the ward, stopping every now and then to peer at her young patients. She halted at the end of Lee's bed. 'Are you all right?'

'I'm fine.'

She came and felt his forehead. 'Not cold any more?'

'No.'

'*Très bien*.' She beamed at him. 'You have a visitor.'

Jeff hobbled out of the shadows on a pair of crutches. 'How do you feel now?' he asked, lowering himself awkwardly on to the end of Lee's bed.

Lee smiled. 'Not so bad. You?'

'I'll live.'

Lee studied his brother's face in the half-light. He looked older and very weary. 'I'm sorry about all the trouble I've caused, Jeff. And thanks for …'

Jeff held up his hand to stop Lee. 'We've all survived. That's the main thing.'

'Yes, but …'

'Nobody's to blame. There's been freak weather this year, that's why it happened.' Jeff reached over and patted Lee's shoulder. 'And next winter, you and Tom will have to come and stay with me again.'

Lee shook his head. 'I'm not sure. I think I've had enough of snow for a while.'

'No way. Don't let one bad experience put you off doing something you enjoy.'

'But …'

'I mean it, Lee. And anyway, Dominique says you're good at snowboarding. A natural. You shouldn't give it up.'

The nurse bustled towards them. 'You must go now,' she said. 'Lee needs to sleep.'

Jeff stood up. He squeezed Lee's hand that was resting outside the bed sheets. 'See you in the morning.'

As he disappeared into the shadows, Lee thought about what Jeff had said … perhaps he *would* come back to Chambeau next year.

With a sigh of contentment, he drifted into sleep.

AVALANCHES

THE ESSENTIAL SURVIVAL GUIDE

People who live near mountains have learned to fear avalanches or the 'white death', as they are known.

The spectacular freefall of thousands of cubic metres of snow, ice, rock and even uprooted trees down a mountainside is a terrifying experience.

If you are caught in an avalanche, you can expect:

A mass of snow and ice heading towards you at incredible speed

●

Stinging snow and grit rammed into your ears, eyes, nose and mouth

●

To be tumbled about and bounced off the mountain slope, which will leave you disorientated

●

To be buried alive, struggling for air and with limited ability to move

●

A very poor chance of survival if not dug out within thirty minutes

YOU CANNOT OUTRUN AN AVALANCHE

Warnings

You can reliably avoid avalanches by recognizing and steering clear of avalanche terrain.

There are four factors that lead to an avalanche:
1. A steep slope of more than twenty-five degrees
2. A snow cover
3. A weak layer in the snow cover
4. A trigger

You can stay safe by travelling:
● At the bottom of valleys, away from large avalanche runouts where snow may be expected to collect
● Along ridgetops, out of reach of avalanches
● In densely wooded areas, where the trees may stop the force of an avalanche
● On slopes of twenty-five degrees or less that do not have steeper slopes above them

LISTEN out for avalanche and severe weather warnings on radio and television.

LEARN to recognize when snow is firmly packed down and therefore safe.

AVOID skiing or snowboarding off-piste on ungroomed trails.

READ up on avalanche safety and take a course on how to identify dangerous conditions.

Be Prepared!

Surviving avalanches can depend on luck, so it is always better to avoid them in the first place. Only one in three victims buried without an avalanche transceiver or beacon survives. If you do intend to travel in avalanche terrain, to minimize risk you should:

● Always take a partner

● Climb, descend or cross avalanche areas one at a time

● Cross suspect slopes at the top or bottom

● Go up or down the edge of a suspect slope rather than through the centre – the likely path of any avalanche

● Carry avalanche rescue equipment such as an avalanche transceiver (*see right*) and a shovel

● Carry a cellular phone with live batteries

● Carry a probe pole, either in the form of a collapsible probe or convertible ski pole

● Stay alert to changing weather conditions

4

Aftermath

If you are caught in an avalanche:

Shout out so your group knows you need help.

Try to get rid of unnecessary equipment. Saving your life is more important than saving your gear.

Fight to stay on the surface. Making swimming motions with your arms will help you stay on top of the snow.

As the avalanche slows, try to get a hand above the surface so that it can be seen.

Cup your other hand over your mouth and nose to give you enough space to breathe.

If you survive the ride and are buried completely, suffocation will become your biggest problem. Avalanche debris is not light and fluffy – even if it started out that way. The moving snow creates heat and friction, which makes it set like concrete the instant it comes to a standstill.

It's unlikely that you will be able to dig yourself out. Try to relax and conserve energy.

If somebody else has been buried, you are their best hope of survival.

If you are part of a group, the most experienced person should take a moment to organize a search party.

Mark the place where you last saw the victim or victims with a ski pole or something equally visible.

If a group of you is searching for an avalanche victim:

● Spread out at intervals to cover the affected area

● Probe in snow around any surface clues – a hand, hat or glove

● Concentrate on the last few metres of the debris from the avalanche and other large piles of snow

● If you go for help, mark your route so the rescue party can follow it back

Avalanches
– The Facts

Where?

Avalanches can occur in all regions of heavy snow with slopes of twenty-five degrees or more that are above the treeline. However, avalanches can also run on slopes well below the treeline, for example, in gullies, road cuts or areas where trees are less dense.

When?

Avalanche danger increases with major snowstorms and periods of thaw. In the Northern Hemisphere, they are most common towards the end of the skiing season – in late February or March. In the Southern Hemisphere they occur most often in August and September.

How?

An avalanche occurs when a layer of snow loses its grip on a slope and slides downhill. A fresh snowfall on top of old and gradually weakening snow is the typical precursor to an avalanche. Many are triggered by their victims – either by the weight of a skier or climber, or by vibrations caused by loud noises.

Effect?

Avalanches are one of the most dangerous natural disasters. The billowing mass of snow, ice and rock will flow downhill on a cushion of air at exceptional speed and flatten almost anything in its path. In highly populated areas this can result in a large loss of life.

Types of Avalanche

Loose-fall Avalanches

This type of avalanche, also called a Sluff avalanche, generally occurs at the surface of new snow or wet spring snow. Sluffs spread out as they tumble downhill, but seldom accumulate enough snow to bury a person very deeply.

Formation of a Loose-fall Avalanche

1 Medium-density snow   2 Lower-density snow
3 Very weak layer, composed of much larger snow crystals
4 Base layer of firm, high-density snow

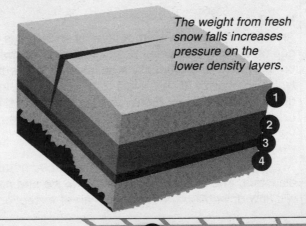

The weight from fresh snow falls increases pressure on the lower density layers.

Ice-fall Avalanches

These occur when a glacier falls down a steep slope. Chunks of ice drop off as the glacier slowly flows downhill under the force of gravity. Ice-fall avalanches are unrelated to temperature, the time of day or any other factor except gravity and weight.

Cornice-fall Avalanches

The snow that forms cornices is very dense and hard, but can be extremely fragile. Cornices look like frozen ocean waves along ridges. Cornice-fall avalanches occur when an overhanging mass of snow breaks loose from a ridge on the leeward slopes of mountainsides.

Poor adhesion between layers 3 and 4 causes the top layers to move

The weak and unstable nature of level 3 now means that the entire slab above can slip down the mountainside

Avalanche Danger Scale

American and European avalanche danger scales rate avalanche hazard in similar ways – except in their use of slightly different colour codes.

LOW HAZARD

Green in both scales
● The snowpack is generally stable, with only isolated areas of instability
Natural or human-triggered avalanches unlikely
Backcountry travel is fairly safe

MODERATE HAZARD

Yellow in both scales
Some areas of instability
Natural avalanches unlikely; human-triggered ones possible
Backcountry travel is possible with caution

CONSIDERABLE HAZARD

Orange in American scale, ochre in European scale
Unstable areas probable
● Natural avalanches possible; human-triggered ones probable
● Backcountry travel is possible with considerable caution

10

HIGH HAZARD

Red in American scale, orange in European scale

Unstable areas highly likely on various slopes

Natural and human-triggered avalanches highly likely

Backcountry travellers should avoid steep and very windy slopes

EXTREME HAZARD

Black in American scale, red in European scale

Extremely unstable layers in snowpack

Natural and human-triggered avalanches are certain

Large destructive avalanches probable

● Backcountry travellers should exercise extreme caution. Avoid any steeply angled terrain or known avalanche areas

Frostbite

Should you survive the initial slide, one of the many dangers avalanches bring with them is frostbite. Frostbite develops as a result of prolonged exposure to temperatures below freezing (zero degrees Celcius or thirty-two degrees Fahrenheit). Uncovered areas of the body are most likely to suffer frostbite, with the nose, ears, cheeks, fingers and toes most often affected.

There are three stages: frostnip, superficial frostbite and deep frostbite.

A foot severely affected by deep frostbite

Frostnip results in a pins and needles feeling in the affected area and the skin turning unusually white and soft. There is no permanent damage. Frostnip can be treated at home by blowing warm breath on the frostnipped area or soaking the area in warm water.

Superficial frostbite causes the skin to feel waxy, frozen, numb and to possibly blister. The skin freezes and ice crystals form inside the skin cells, but the tissue underneath remains flexible.

Deep frostbite requires prompt medical attention to prevent infection and the possible loss of a limb. It affects the blood vessels, muscles, nerves, tendons and even the bone. It may lead to permanent damage, blood clots and sometimes gangrene. The affected areas will become completely numb to all feeling.

Hypothermia

People who have been buried in an avalanche get very cold and can suffer from hypothermia. Sometimes referred to as 'exposure', hypothermia is a lowering of the inner body core temperature below thirty-five degrees Celsius. It is dangerous and requires immediate medical care.

Hypothermia is considered moderate if the body temperature is between thirty-five and thirty-two degrees, serious between thirty-two and twenty-five degrees and major under twenty-five degrees.

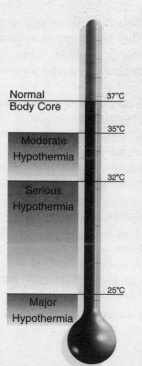

Normal Body Core — 37°C

35°C — Moderate Hypothermia

32°C — Serious Hypothermia

25°C — Major Hypothermia

13

Hypothermia affects victims differently depending on their physical condition, the reason for their loss of temperature, and the rate of its onset.

Hypothermia is indicated by:
- Confusion or sleepiness
- Slow, slurred speech or shallow breathing
- Weak pulse
- Low blood pressure
- Excessive shivering

Sub-chronic hypothermia
This hypothermia is found in poor urban environments in winter. Onset is slow and affects older people more often than younger people.

Sub-acute hypothermia
This hypothermia is typical of an unharmed traveller stuck on a mountain. It only appears when the body's energy reserves are used up. Onset is more or less rapid according to the patient's condition and state of exhaustion.

Acute hypothermia
This kind of hypothermia occurs in injured skiers immobilized in snow, a crevasse or freezing water. The victim must be very carefully extricated, insulated, immobilized, possibly sedated and very carefully transferred to hospital.

Avalanches
– The Biggies

Place: The Italian Alps
Date: October 218 BC
Effects: Hannibal's crossing of the Alps into Italy began with an army of 38,000 soldiers, 8,000 horses and thirty-seven elephants. On the first day of his journey, the weather was terrible. His troops and animals were forced to camp for two days on a mountain pass to sit out the storm. On the third day, Hannibal decided to continue the march. Deep layers of newly fallen snow covered the old icy-hard snow. As the convoy began to traverse down the mountain, the animals sank down to the old snow. In no time at all, the bottom snow layer began to give way. Hannibal tested it by piercing it with his lance but, as he did so, the whole snow layer moved. A great part of his army plunged off the mountain as the avalanche overwhelmed them. A number of the elephants, 2,000 horses and 18,000 men fell to their deaths.

Place: Elm, Switzerland
Date: 11 September 1881
Effect: One Sunday afternoon, the top of the Plattenberg Kopf mountain slid down on to the village of Elm. After years of work, miners had undermined the peak by digging at the rocks below. It took sev-

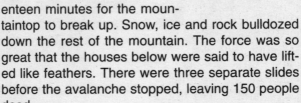

enteen minutes for the mountaintop to break up. Snow, ice and rock bulldozed down the rest of the mountain. The force was so great that the houses below were said to have lifted like feathers. There were three separate slides before the avalanche stopped, leaving 150 people dead.

Place: Wellington, Washington State, USA
Date: 1 March 1910
Effect: For nine days in February, a blizzard hit the Cascade mountains in Washington State. The railway was cut off as huge amounts of snow – up to three and a half metres (eleven feet) – drifted across the region every day. Many people were stranded, among them 100 passengers in a train at a settlement in Wellington. Finally, on 28 February, the snow stopped falling and warm winds blew in. The heavy snow gradually became more unstable and began to move. At 1.00 a.m., a

16

huge ridge of snow, seven metres high and half a kilometre wide, plunged from a mountain towards Wellington. The wall of snow smashed into the train where the passengers were sleeping. In seconds the train, the buildings near by and the rails were thrown into a thirty-metre-deep gorge. Within a minute the avalanche stopped. Only twenty-six people were rescued. There were ninety-six deaths.

Place: Galcier 511, Mount Huascaran, The Andes
Date: 10 January 1962
Effect: Glacier 511, at over 7,000 metres (21,000 feet), cracked and slid down the mountainside with spectacular effect. The avalanche was so huge that when it was first seen it was thought to be a cloud. An enormous 3 million tonnes of ice raced through the valley below and swallowed

17

flocks of sheep, soil, rocks and trees. It reached a speed of 90 kmph (60 mph) and grew to a height of twenty metres. The town of Ranrahirea was crushed. All that remained after it was hit was a jumble of ruins, mud and ice. Only one person in the town survived. The death toll reached 3,500.

Place: Val d'Isere, French Alps
Date: 10 February 1970
Effect: A terrible snowstorm struck the resort in early February. Thousands of tons of snow collected on the 3,000 metre Dome. When it came down, the avalanche swept through the dining room of a hostel where people were just having breakfast.

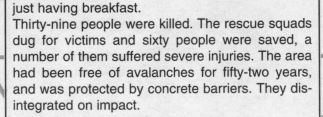

Thirty-nine people were killed. The rescue squads dug for victims and sixty people were saved, a number of them suffered severe injuries. The area had been free of avalanches for fifty-two years, and was protected by concrete barriers. They disintegrated on impact.

Place: Rechingen, Switzerland
Date: 24 February 1970
Effect: A gigantic avalanche bombarded this

Swiss army base in 1970. Five chalets in the army camp were hit directly and a three-storey officers' mess was completely destroyed. Though the rescue by the remaining experienced army teams began at once, only eighteen people were rescued alive. Some of the survivors were badly injured. The snow continued, reaching knee height, making the rescue more difficult. The last survivor was found after five days.

Astounding!

Avalanche Facts

The greatest natural avalanches are rarely seen – they tend to happen in uninhabited parts of the Himalayas.

Eighty-nine per cent of all avalanche victims are men.

At the site of the 1836 avalanche at Lewes in East Sussex, England, the event was commemorated by the opening of a pub called The Snowdrop Inn.

In 1984 in Columbia, an ice sheet was melted by the eruption of the Peligro volcano. The combination of the avalanche and the volcanic eruption left a layer of debris several hundred metres thick. 20,000 people were killed.

Permanent snow and ice covers about one eighth of the Earth's land surface – approximately 21 million square kilometres.

The fastest avalanche in a populated area struck at Glarnisch in Switzerland on 6 March 1898. It travelled at 349 kmph (217 mph). It covered nearly seven kilometres (just over four miles) in one minute.